REVENGE of the ITTY-BITTY BROTHERS

For Ben,
I hope this
tickles your
funny bone!

Lin Oliver

HA HA

Also by Lin Oliver

WHO SHRUNK DANIEL FUNK?:

WHO SHRUNK DANIEL FUNK?:

WHO SHRUNK DANIEL FUNK?:

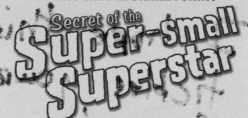

WHO SHRUNK DANIEL FUNK?

BOOK 3

REVENGE of the ITTY-BITTY BROTHERS

Written by Lin Oliver
Illustrated by Stephen Gilpin

Simon & Schuster Books for Young Readers
New York   London   Toronto   Sydney

SIMON & SCHUSTER BOOKS FOR YOUNG READERS
An imprint of Simon & Schuster Children's Publishing Division
1230 Avenue of the Americas, New York, New York 10020
This book is a work of fiction. Any references to historical events, real people, or real locales are used fictitiously. Other names, characters, places, and incidents are products of the author's imagination, and any resemblance to actual events or locales or persons, living or dead, is entirely coincidental.
Text copyright © 2009 by Lin Oliver
Illustrations copyright © 2009 by Stephen Gilpin
All rights reserved, including the right of reproduction in whole or in part in any form.
SIMON & SCHUSTER BOOKS FOR YOUNG READERS is a trademark of Simon & Schuster, Inc.
For information about special discounts for bulk purchases, please contact Simon & Schuster Special Sales at 1-866-506-1949 or business@simonandschuster.com.
The Simon & Schuster Speakers Bureau can bring authors to your live event. For more information or to book an event, contact the Simon & Schuster Speakers Bureau at 1-866-248-3049 or visit our website at www.simonspeakers.com.
Also available in a Simon & Schuster Books for Young Readers hardcover edition.
Book design by Chloë Foglia
The text of this book is set in Minister.
The illustrations for this book are rendered in ink.
Manufactured in the United States of America
0410 OFF
First Simon & Schuster Books for Young Readers paperback edition March 2010
10 9 8 7 6 5 4 3 2
The Library of Congress has cataloged the hardcover edition as follows:
Oliver, Lin.
Revenge of the itty-bitty brothers / written by Lin Oliver ; illustrated by Stephen Gilpin. —1st ed.
p. cm.—(Who shrunk Daniel Funk? ; bk. #3)
Summary: When Daniel learns to control his shrinking, Pablo, his tiny twin, writes a list of fun things they can do, including riding in a model rocket near the La Brea Tar Pits, which teaches the brothers the importance of sticking together.
ISBN 978-1-4169-0961-3 (hc)
[1. Size—Fiction. 2. Brothers and sisters—Fiction. 3. Rockets (Aeronautics)—Fiction. 4. Family life—Fiction. 5. Twins—Fiction. 6. La Brea Pits (Calif.)—Fiction. 7. Humorous stories] I. Gilpin, Stephen, ill. II. Title
PZ7.O476Rev 2009
[Fic]—dc22
2008030231
ISBN 978-1-4169-0962-0 (pbk)
ISBN 978-1-4169-9524-1 (eBook)

In memory of my mother, Unnie Oliver, who brought me up to read and to laugh ... the perfect combo—L. O.

For Makena. She knows a thing or two about little brothers now—S. G.

ACKNOWLEDGMENTS

Hey, pals. I have manners, you know. I never burp in public unless I think my stomach is going to explode, and I always say thank you for birthday presents, even the ones I don't like such as button-down shirts and white underpants. So just to show off my excellent manners, I'm right here and now giving a HUGE shout out to everyone who helped me make this book. Oh, you know who you are. That's right, David Gale and Navah Wolfe, I mean you. And you too, Ellen Goldsmith-Vein and Kim Turrisi. And don't try to pretend you're not a huge support team, you guys at the SCBWI office and also those four fabuloso Baker boys, Alan, Cole, Oliver, and Theo. You all get the biggest thumbs-up ever from me.

The Funkster

And thanks from me, too. Hey, he's not the only Funk with manners!

The Pablo

DANIEL

PABLO

LARK

VU

GREAT GRANNY NANNY

THE CAST OF CHARACTERS

REVENGE of the ITTY-BITTY BROTHERS

Hey, great news!

I just learned what a prologue is.

Okay, so maybe you're not jumping up and down in your size seven Nikes, hooting and hollering and shouting, "Three cheers for this guy, he's learned what a prologue is." (By the way, if you *are* doing that, close this book right now, because that's a really weird thing to do and you need to go to a doctor immediately and get that checked out.)

Now, put yourself in my place. Here I am writing a prologue again, but *this* time, I actually know what one is, which is definitely cool. I might not have ever found out, except that a bunch of you wrote me letters after my first book and said, "Hey, ding-dong . . . why not try learning what a prologue is before you go and write one?" If you ask me, and I know you didn't, that was an excellent suggestion.

So I took your advice and got out the big old dictionary my sister Lark keeps next to her pillow. (That's right, she likes to fall asleep *reading the dictionary*, which, by the way, I consider highly and completely and totally abnormal, like everything else my three sisters do.) And there it was on page

362, right after "prolix" and just before "prolong."

Prologue—an introduction to a poem, play, or literary work.

Literary work! I like the sound of that. This isn't just a book you're reading, my friends. It's a *literary work*. Hey, are we smart or what?

Now I don't mean to turn this into a big, boring, brain-twisting vocab lesson or anything, but there's one other word that you're going to need.

Giccup.

If you're the "I love to read dictionaries" type like my sister Lark, go right ahead and look it up. Knock yourself out. But I'm warning you, I doubt that you'll find it, because I'm pretty sure it's a word I made up myself. So I'll just tell you right now what a giccup is and save your eyes from having to squint at all those ant-sized words crawling around on those humungous dictionary pages.

Have you ever taken a big swig of Coke and right afterward, without even thinking about it, opened your mouth to say something and a huge burp came flying out? Don't try to tell me that's never happened to you. I know it has, because it's happened to me like a thousand times. Anyway, that sound is *not* a giccup. It's a burp, which is a first cousin to a giccup.

Question Number Two. Have you ever gotten a

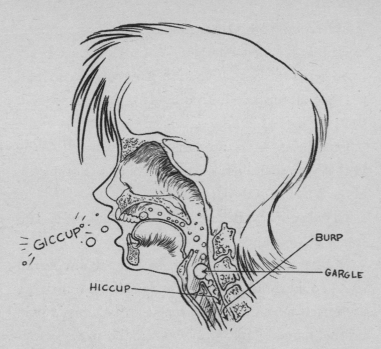

GICCUP

HICCUP

BURP

GARGLE

really big case of the hiccups, like after you've eaten a spicy burrito from a bad fast-food drive-thru? And then your whole family starts waving their hands in your face and screaming BOO to try to scare you and make the hiccups go away? Well, those hiccups are related to giccups, but still not the real deal.

Last question. Have you ever gargled with mouthwash? My mom makes me do it when I have a sore throat. You take a mouthful of the stuff, then tilt your head way back and try to say something starting with G, like "great green gobs of goofy grapes." Then two things happen. First, you feel like a total jerk. Second, your throat makes this weird bubbling noise that is called a gargle.

So here's the deal. If you mix a burp, a hiccup, and a gargle all together into one giant slobbery sound, that, my friends, is a giccup.

Okay, now you're probably asking yourself, "Why is this guy spending a whole prologue rattling on about a slobbery throat sound?"

I'll tell you why. Because last Thursday, one giccup totally changed my life.

Maybe not quite as much as when I discovered that I could shrink down to the size of the fourth toe on my left foot. Or when I realized that I had a twin brother named Pablo who was also the size of a toe.

But still, that giccup was a very very big deal.

You'll see. When I tell you what happened last Thursday at 3:47 p.m. right after I giccuped in Science Club, you're going to say, "Daniel Funk, you have *got* to be kidding!"

Oh, yeah: Daniel Funk, that's me. Welcome to my world.

CHAPTER 1

The Funkster's Funky Fact #1:
Astronauts in space cannot burp.

"What's up with your stomach, man?" my best friend, Vu Tran, whispered to me. "It sounds like you swallowed a sick frog."

"I think it was that taco I ate for a snack," I said, pressing my stomach up against the edge of the table to try to quiet the rumbling. "It's kicking up a fuss in there."

It was last Thursday after school, and we were in Ms. Addison's science room, putting the finishing touches on the model rockets we had been building in Science Club. I was almost done making the Screamin' Mimi, a very cool black and silver rocket that actually whistles when it flies. Vu was putting decals on his Big Bertha, which is a more basic rocket but all in all, still a very solid choice.

My stomach rumbled again, this time even louder.

"You eat tacos all the time," Vu said, stopping work to give my midsection a suspicious glance. "And they've never sounded like that."

"Yeah, well, this taco had some personal problems.

Like I brought it for lunch on Tuesday and it's been sitting in my locker since then."

"You ate a three-day-old taco from your locker?" my sister Robin piped up from across the room. "Honestly, Daniel, why don't you just eat from the garbage can?"

Leave it to the big ears of Robin Flamingo Funk to pick up on anything negative that's going on with me. She's like a one-person "let's dump on Daniel" machine. Man, was I sorry she had heard this piece of old taco info.

Robin gave me a disgusted look and rolled her eyes so far back in her head I thought they were going to disappear into her skull. I stared her down, though, and just drilled my eyeballs directly into her face. I didn't even blink. Finally, she went back to painting her model rocket, which, by the way, was hot pink, to match her phone and her toenails and her iPod and her camera and her toothbrush and everything else she owns. It's a known fact that the only reason Robin signed up for Science Club in the first place was because she wanted to learn how to make pink bubble gum–scented lip gloss.

I was hopeful my stare down would end the taco conversation, but no. When Robin is on a dump-on-Daniel roll, there's no stopping her. After a minute, she glanced over at me for no good reason at all and muttered, "A three-day-old taco. What were you thinking, Daniel?"

"It's not like there was anything growing on it," I snapped. "Okay, the lettuce was brownish but I picked most of it off. And so what if the cheese smelled like gym socks. I happen to like the aroma of sports gear."

Robin pretended she was gagging. Or maybe she actually was, which would have been sweet.

"Daniel, you are grossest person in the known world," she said.

That did it. If Robin was going to talk trash about me, I'd give her something to talk about. I have my breaking point, you know.

"Hey Robs, you want to see something gross? Check this out."

I pulled down my lower lip and showed her the big juicy blister I had gotten from shoving an entire piece of scorching hot microwave pizza into my mouth all at once.

"Eeuuww," Robin said, catching a glimpse of my inner lip, which, I confess, doesn't look so good even without the blister. "I might actually barf."

"Now who's gross?" I said, giving Vu a high five as we laughed like a couple of ticklish hyenas.

Wouldn't you know it, Vince Bruno walked by at that very second, just when Vu and I were at the height of acting like total idiots. Trust me, guys—Vince Bruno is definitely not the person you want to act like a total idiot around. He cuts you no slack. I mean zero.

"You two nerd balls cracking up over a stupid blister?" he said, shaking his tomato-shaped head in disgust. "Imagine what you'd do if you saw something really gross, like I did last night in my restaurant."

Oh yeah, like *he* owns the restaurant. Just because his dad owns a whole bunch of Pizza Kings, Vince acts like he's the total Prince of Pizza. He never misses an opportunity to brag about how rich his family is and how many restaurants they own.

By the way—I think their crusts are soggy, and it's a known fact that they skimp on the pepperoni.

"This little kid ordered the special double-cheese-and-garlic pizza," he said, "and ate three huge slices. Then he barfed them up right into his SpongeBob backpack."

Vince burst out laughing. Vu and I just stared at him. I mean, I have a pretty good sense of humor, but if you ask me, and I know you didn't, I don't see what's so funny about a little kid upchucking his dinner. But this obviously tickled old Vince's funny bone, and he laughed with such force, I thought his breath was going to blow my Screamin' Mimi off my desk and into orbit.

"I'm glad you boys find model rocket building so funny," Ms. Addison said, walking over to our table, where Vince was still belting out his monster laugh. "I like my Science Club members to be happy."

She's really nice, that Ms. Addison, which is the main reason I keep signing up for Science Club. Actually, it's the second main reason. The first reason is because we get to touch worms and jellyfish and sea cucumbers and other slimy things. I like to pick them up and jiggle them under Robin's nose.

I don't get why girls are so grossed out by a little slime. I mean, I have three sisters and they're all totally different. Lark, who's fifteen, is obsessed with writing so-called poetry for her blog, www.I'm-a-freak.com, which is read by exactly no one. Robin, who's fourteen and otherwise known as Miss I-Totally-Love-Everything-Pink, spends her entire day either on her pink phone or practicing standing in front of the mirror looking cute in her pink volleyball uniform. Goldie, who's seven and a half, is a Barbie fanatic whose idea of a good time is tripping around the house in my mom's high-heeled shoes. But even though the three of them are completely different, I can tell you this:

One thing they have in common is that they all hate slimy things.

I know this for a fact, because I personally have placed a slug in each of their beds. You've never heard screaming like that in your whole life. It was awesome.

"Vince, please take a seat at your table," Ms. Addison said. "I'll be there to check your rocket in a minute."

"You don't have to," Vince answered in his usual obnoxious way. "My dad bought me the most expensive model in the catalogue. It's going to blow these baby toys out of the water."

"Spending a lot of money isn't always the answer," Ms. Addison said to him. And even though I didn't say anything to her, I thought to myself, *You are a rock star, Ms. Addison!*

"So, Daniel," she said to me as Vince went off in a sulk. "Do you think your rocket is ready for the launch?"

"You bet. Screamin' Mimi here is going straight to the moon. And she's going to be whistling all the way."

"I'll be happy if she just clears the treetops in the park," Ms. Addison said, checking to see that the glue was dry on my tail fins. Then she turned to the class and added, "Remember, everyone, we're meet-

ing for the launch Saturday at eleven o'clock in La Brea Park, right next to the tar pits. Bring your rocket and pack a lunch."

I was pretty excited about the rocket launch. I needed a chance to rebuild my reputation from the first launch, which . . . let's just say . . . didn't go so well for me. In the fall session of Science Club, I had built a super cool-looking Big Bertha that I painted red with black decals. When we launched our rockets in the park, everyone else's rocket went straight up in the air—but not mine. Nope, my Big Bertha took off sideways, made only one pathetic circle, barely six inches off the ground, then bamo-slamo, crashed into one of the tar pits.

Holy macaroni, that was sad. I could hear old Bertha bubbling as she sank all the way down into the tar. The only thing louder was Vince Bruno laughing up a storm. Leave it to Vince the Pizza Prince, who, you've probably figured out by now, is a world-class jerk, to make fun of someone whose first rocket had just nose-dived.

By the way, if you're wondering what a tar pit is, I don't blame you. I'm willing to bet that your neighborhood park doesn't have huge bubbling pits of sticky black tar scattered around it. But Hancock Park, which is in the middle of Los Angeles and about seven miles from where I live in Venice, California, does. They're called the La Brea Tar Pits, and scientists have actually discovered a ton of bones buried there from prehistoric creatures like woolly mammoths and saber-toothed tigers and dire wolves who got stuck in that tar and died a bazillion years ago. The park even has a museum with real skeletons and bones of all those prehistoric animals. Ms. Addison likes to hold our rocket launches there so we can cruise around and look in those pits. That shows you just how nice a teacher she is.

Anyway, back in Science Club, Ms. Addison was

testing my nose cone to make sure it was a tight fit. And wouldn't you know it, my stomach did the froggy noise again. Big time. It sounded like there was a whole pond full of sick frogs croaking in my guts. Ms. Addison tried to ignore it, but when a guy's stomach is growling like a herd of frogs, it's a hard thing to ignore. I looked over at Vu, and we both had to stuff our fists into our mouths to keep from bursting out laughing.

Ms. Addison looked like she was going to laugh too. Quickly, she hightailed it away from our table and over to where Arthur Krems was working on his Saturn 5. I couldn't really blame her. I wouldn't want to listen to my stomach noises, either.

"You've got to do something about that, man," Vu said, after Ms. Addison was out of earshot.

"Like what?"

"Maybe if you burped, things would quiet down. Relieve a little of the gas build-up, if you know what I mean."

I certainly did know what he meant. I am something of a burping expert. I have been known to produce a burp that lasts eleven seconds, which is no easy thing to accomplish.

My grandma Lola, who teaches world culture, is a big believer in burping after a meal. She says that the Bengalis over in India, actually consider it a compliment to the cook if you burp after a meal. The louder you burp, the better the meal. If you ask me, and I know you didn't, I think those Bengalis know a thing or two about human digestion. I give them a big thumbs-up.

I also happen to know that here in the United States, it is definitely not okay to burp in the middle of Science Club. I wasn't raised in a barn, you know.

"Will you excuse me, Vu?" I said with a little fake bow. "I have an urgent matter to take care of in the hall."

"You are most definitely excused," Vu said, bowing back.

"May I go to the bathroom, Ms. Addison," I called out.

"Certainly, Daniel," she said, without even looking up. I think she was relieved. The herd of frogs in my belly had clued her in that I was having, let's just say, a stomach issue.

I walked out into the hall and looked around. No one was there. It was after school and everyone but us science nuts had gone home.

Okay, Daniel. Here's your chance. Let one rip.

I took in a big gulp of air and tried to burp, but nothing came out. I tried again, and still nothing.

Finally, I walked over to the water fountain and drank a ton of water really fast, purposely swallowing lots of air as I did. If that didn't make me burp, nothing would.

I must not have completely swallowed all the water, because when I tried to burp again, what came out was a combination of a burp and a hiccup and a watery gargle.

And if you were paying attention during the prologue, I know that you know what that was.

Yup. I let out a world-class giccup.

(And this, my friends, is why we read prologues.)

Immediately after the giccup, my stomach felt much better. The rumbling and the grumbling magically stopped.

But something else way weirder happened.

My eyeballs started to growl.

My nose felt like it was blowing bubbles.

My fingers began to buzz.

And sure enough, my knees let out a whistling sound.

Oh no! Was I shrinking? Right here in the hall? In the middle of Science Club?

This was not good.

CHAPTER 2

The Funkster's Funky Fact #2: Most dust particles in your house are made from dried dead skin.

Yup, I was shrinking all right.

In fact, not only was I shrinking, I was shrinking fast. In one second, I had gone from a relatively normal (size-wise anyway) sixth-grader to the size of a toe. I know this because when my eyeballs first started to growl, I happened to look up at the big hall clock. It said 3:47 and the second hand was on thirty-two. By the time my knees stopped whistling, the second hand was on thirty-three. I'm no math brainiac, but I subtract well enough to know that one second had elapsed.

My head was spinning like a top. I'm sorry for complaining. I don't mean to sound like a wuss, but you try shrinking over four feet in one second and see if your head doesn't spin too.

As the hall gradually stopped swirling around me, I rubbed my eyes and checked out my surroundings. Lots of huge green walls, rows of fluorescent lights way, way, way up there on the ceiling, and . . . uh-oh.

Something was walking down the linoleum floor toward me, something big and red and ugly. What was that thing?

I looked at it carefully. Holy macaroni! It was a red ant. He was half my size and I swear, looked like a man-eating monster from a really scary horror movie. He stopped when he saw me and twitched his

antennae in a way that definitely told me he didn't want to be my new best friend.

"Shoo, boy," I said. That was weak and I knew it.

Obviously, Mr. Ant didn't like my attitude. He twitched his antennae again and I knew he was considering biting me. At my size, one bite from him would take a considerable chunk out of my thigh.

I flashed him my friendliest grin and took a real casual tone of voice.

"Nice ant," I said. "I like your color. Red looks good on you."

My heart was pumping hard and inside I was thinking, *Please, angel of red biting ants. Make him not like boy flesh. Make him go back to his mound or hive or hole or wherever red ants live.*

Here's a tip: If you ever shrink to the size of a toe and see a gigantic red ant coming at you, looking like he's going to bite your leg off, don't get all aggressive with him. Just flash him a smile and a friendly wave.

I'm telling you this because luckily, that strategy worked for me. The ant stared at me for longer than I was really comfortable with, then just took off down the hall on his six beefy legs. Oh, you don't think ant legs are beefy? Trust me, they are when you're the size of a toe.

As he strolled down the hall, I let out a giant sigh

of relief. The more distance between him and me, the better. I hustled about a hundred steps in the other direction, but I could tell I hadn't covered much, because the water fountain was still above me. It was like a huge metal mountain looming over my head. A drop of icy water leaked out of its pipe and before I could run for cover, it landed on me, soaking me. Brrrr, that was cold.

The freezing water cleared my foggy brain, though, and brought me to my senses. What was going on? Why had I suddenly shrunk, with no warning?

For the past two weeks, ever since that Tuesday when I shrank for the first time, we had been trying to figure out what caused it. By we, I mean Great Granny Nanny, who is my dad's grandma, and me. She's the only one besides my brother, Pablo, who knows about my . . . uh . . . shrinking problem. In fact, she's the only one besides me who knows about Pablo.

Granny Nanny believes that what's making me shrink is her goulash, which is a very goopy beef stew she learned to make from her grandma. She's been feeding me weird combinations of goulash meat and carrots and fish eggs and seaweed every time I open my mouth. Sometimes I shrink after I eat it. But sometimes nothing at all happens.

Which tells me it's not the goulash.

Pablo believes that I can make myself shrink just by concentrating really hard.

"Dude," he told me the other day, "wrap your brain around it. Think small. You can do it, Pruitt."

Then he fell asleep in my little sister Goldie's Barbie Jacuzzi, where he likes to hang out. (He also likes lying on a cotton ball or kicking back in the paper clip box on my desk.) I sat there in front of the Barbie Dream House, thinking small thoughts. Puppy teeth. Pin heads. Fleas. Nanobots. Really, really sharp pencil points. Nothing happened, except that I did creep Goldie out when she found me sitting cross-legged in front of her Barbie bathroom.

Another drop leaked from the water fountain pipe. Before I could get out of the way, it plopped onto my head, sending shivers down my itty-bitty spine and a new question into my itty-bitty brain. What was I going to do now?

If I didn't unshrink myself before Science Club ended, Ms. Addison would come looking for me. I definitely didn't want that, because it's very hard to explain to your science teacher, especially a really nice one, that sometimes you turn into a miniguy the size of the fourth toe on your left foot.

I had to make myself sneeze. Even though I don't

know what makes me shrink, I do know what makes me un-shrink, and that's sneezing. So I wiggled my nose like a bunny rabbit with itchy whiskers and opened my mouth wide.

"Ah . . . ah . . . ah . . . ah chooooo!" I hollered at the top of my voice.

I waited. Nothing happened. I remained the size of a toe.

Okay, I confess: It was a fake sneeze. And when we're talking about unshrinking yourself, fake sneezes don't work. You can't just say "achoo" really loud and blow some air out of your nose and some spit out of your mouth. It has to be an honest-to-goodness actual sneeze.

The problem was, I didn't feel like sneezing. No itch in the nose. No tickle in the nostril. None of that action.

Sneezing is a weird thing. It seems like you always sneeze when you don't want to, like when you're at the dentist getting your teeth cleaned, or when you're getting your hair cut and those little snippets of hair are flying up the old nostrils. But try to sneeze when you really want to, and you'll find it's harder than you think.

Luck was with me. Coming down the hall at just that very second was Mr. Mintz, our school custodian.

He was pushing a wide broom and on the bristles was just what I was hoping to see. It was a row of dust balls the size of Jupiter, mixed in with all kinds of other sneeze-producing crud like shreds of paper and bits of hair and . . . well, I'll stop now, so I don't gross you out entirely.

LIN OLIVER

I knew what I had to do. I took a deep breath and ran smack into the broom, diving head first into a giant dust ball filled with little black particles of who-knows-what. A bunch of that crud stuck to my wet shirt, but I didn't care. I took a deep breath in, sucking all that dust and black stuff into my nostrils. It worked like a charm.

"Ah . . . ah . . . AH CHOO," I sneezed, this time for real.

Suddenly, there I was, big as life, standing in the hall in a muddy wet shirt, with both feet planted squarely in Mr. Mintz's broom bristles.

"Daniel," he said, looking majorly surprised. "Where did you come from?"

Good question. Wish I had an answer.

"Um . . . over there," I said, pointing to the blank green wall.

"You walked out of the wall?" he said, giving me a suspicious look.

Think fast, Funkster. This isn't working.

"I mean, I came from over there," I said, pointing totally in the other direction. We both looked over to see what was there. Lucky for me, I was pointing to a door this time.

"You came from the supply closet?" he said, scratching his bald head.

Oh, so that's what it was! Great! I could work with that.

"Yeah," I said. "I was looking for a clean shirt. This one got all wet and muddy from . . . uh . . . me falling into a really wet and muddy thingee."

"There are no shirts in the supply closet," he said. "Shirts are not considered supplies."

"You are so right, Mr. Mintz," I said. "And I know that because I'm very involved with supplies. I find supplies excellent to have. One thing you don't ever want to do is run short of supplies."

"But that closet is locked," Mr. Mintz said, going over and pulling on the knob to check that the door didn't open.

"Right again!" I said, "And imagine my disappointment when I discovered I couldn't get any supplies, because now I have a muddy shirt *and* I'm short of supplies, which is never a good combination."

I could feel myself starting to sweat.

"Hey, Dan," said a voice from behind me. "Ms. Addison is asking where you are. Get in here."

It was Vu. Man, was he ever a welcome sight.

"What happened to your shirt?" he said, staring at the clumps of wet dirt hanging off my T-shirt.

"Apparently, he fell in a wet and muddy thingee," Mr. Mintz volunteered.

Thank goodness Vu is not the kind of guy who asks a lot of questions.

"Yeah, I hate it when that happens," was all he said. We thought about that for a second, then I took the opportunity to clear out of there.

"Gee, Mr. Mintz, I'd like to keep chatting with you," I said, "but I'm needed in Science Club. If we're ever going to walk on Mars, I've got to get cracking on that right away. So long, Mr. Mintz."

I turned on my heel and bolted back into class without looking back.

Phew, that was close.

Saved by the Vu.

CHAPTER 3

The Funkster's Funky Fact #3: An Olympic gold medal is made out of 92.5 percent silver.

I didn't get home until almost four-thirty that afternoon, and Pablo was waiting impatiently. The second I walked into my room and tossed my backpack down on my race-car bed, the PabloPhone started to ring. It's not a real phone—it's one we created ourselves out of green plastic straws stuck together into a long tube. When Pablo talks at one end and I put the other end up to my ear, I can hear him as clearly as if he's the same size as me. He rings it by jiggling it in the air.

"Hey, Pabs," I said, flopping down into my blue leather La-Z-Boy chair and flipping the lever into the recline position. "What's up?"

"Everything's up, bro," he said. "The Pablo has put together a fun-filled afternoon for us."

He was standing on my desk, balancing on a yellow number two pencil, trying to stay upright while rolling it with his feet.

"Such as?"

"I have created The Mini Man Olympics," he

said. "And today is Day One of the competition."

That's the great thing about Pablo. He is all fun, all the time. Not like the girls in my house who think an afternoon of fun is trying on different shades of nail polish and then blogging about it.

"Sounds great," I said. "When do we get started?"

"The torch lighting was an hour ago, dude. A certain somebody missed it because that certain somebody came home late."

"I'm sorry, Pablo. I forgot to tell you. Thursday is Science Club day."

Pablo and I have only known each other for two weeks, so he doesn't have my after-school schedule memorized yet. And to tell you the truth, I'm not used to having someone to play with every day after school. It's weird to suddenly have a twin brother. I mean, I've always *had* him, but I didn't *know* about him.

Did I tell you that Great Granny Nanny found him in my ear when I was born, all curled up like a baby kangaroo? I know that sounds creepy, but get used to it, because it's the truth and I always tell the truth, except every now and then when I forget to wash my baseball pants and I turn them inside out and tell the coach they're clean.

Anyway, if you're wondering what Great Granny Nanny was doing poking around in my one-day-old baby ears, let me just say: that makes two of us. One thing I've learned is that you can't explain what grown-ups do. Like sitting around talking after dinner without the TV even on. I ask you, What's the point of *that?*

Great Granny Nanny thinks that maybe we have this shrinking gene in our family. She can't ask my dad about it, because he died on a bird-watching expedition in South America seven years ago. But *her* grandmother told her that way back in the day, when the Funk clan still lived in the old country, there was a little shrinking Funkster. The poor dude got captured and studied by scientists and had to live in a cage and have a miserable life. Because of that, Granny keeps Pablo safe by not telling anyone about him, not even my mom and my sisters.

We have to be really careful because when you live in a house of six women, it's hard to keep anything secret. Just imagine what would happen if Lark the Motor Mouth knew about Pablo—she'd be posting poems about him on her blog, www.I-write-cruddy-poetry.com. Robin would be speed-dialing everyone on her volleyball team to blab about what he was wearing. And Goldie would be bringing in rasp-berry-scented-marker drawings of him for her "I Am Special" day.

Girls. I mean, really.

It's a known fact that if you have a secret in my house, you can just forget about keeping it. Like my wart. I might as well tell you about it, since my sisters let the cat out of the bag anyway. Just don't laugh, okay?

I had this wart on the bottom of my foot when I was seven years old. I was very ashamed of it. At the time, I believed you got warts from touching a frog, and I didn't want everyone in school to think that I had been petting a frog with my foot or anything weird like that.

Hey, I asked you not to laugh, okay? Give me a break. I was just a kid.

Anyway, my mom took me to Dr. Fink (no relation to Funk) and he gave me some cream to make the wart dry up and drop off. (Sorry, if that's too much info, but if you want the truth, it's not always pretty.) Before I had even left Dr. Fink's office, everyone in school knew about my warty foot. Good old Robin had made a get-well card, all decorated up with her usual pink glitter and feathers, and she and Lark passed it around for everyone in school to sign. I'll never forget it. It said,

Got foot warts? Don't you worry!
They'll be gone in a hurry!

They hung it up on my classroom door, which ended any hopes I had of keeping my warty foot problem to myself. For the rest of the year after that, Vince the Pizza Prince Bruno called me "wart hog." And every time we went into his Dad's pizza chain and he was there, he'd ask if I wanted pizza with pepperoni and warts.

Thank you, Robin and Lark.

So, back to Pablo and the Mini Man Olympics.

He really had planned an entire Olympic afternoon.

"Check out the first event," he said into the PabloPhone. "Pencil rolling. It requires balance, skill, and footwork."

Then he rolled the pencil under his feet, being careful never to lose his balance and fall off.

"It looks totally fun," I said.

"It is, bro. But I'm afraid you can't participate. You're over the height limit. If you stepped on one of these pencils, you'd crush it like an eggshell."

"I wish I could shrink whenever I wanted to." I sighed.

"It's all in the mind. Think small, Paul. Now if you'll excuse me, I'm due at the starting line."

Pablo pretended to fire an imaginary starting gun, then took off, executing some really fancy footwork on the pencil. He must have been practicing all day, because he was amazing. He rolled the pencil along the top of my desk, balancing with his arms and propelling it with his feet. He maneuvered around the stapler and my amethyst geode and came to a stop at a yellow highlighter he had set up at the finish line.

"Ta-da!" he said, holding both his arms up in the air. "Gold medal for Pablo Picasso Diego Funk."

He picked up a gold earring of Robin's that was lying on my desk and placed it around his neck.

"Robin would kill you if she knew you swiped her earring," I said.

"One of the many advantages of being small, bro, is that nobody can see you swipe stuff."

"There are disadvantages, too," I said to Pablo. "Like today in Science Club, I shrunk and was almost eaten by a red ant."

Pablo quickly jumped off the yellow pencil and approached me.

"Come down here," he shouted. I put my face right up to the desk so I could hear him without the PabloPhone.

"What happened just before you shrunk?" he asked with an intense voice that was not typical of him. "Was there any goulash involved?"

"No. Why?"

"Any other special foods?"

"No. All I had was a three-day-old taco, about a half-hour before I shrunk."

"That's it? You're sure?"

"Totally positive. I couldn't have possibly eaten anything else because that taco was kicking up a nasty fuss in my stomach."

"What'd you do about it?" I could see Pablo was really interested in this subject. He usually isn't big on asking a lot of questions, especially about my digestive juices.

"I went into the hall, drank a bunch of water, and let out a massive giccup. It was a prizewinner."

"That's *it*!" Pablo shouted. "The Pablo has figured it out!"

"What's *it*? What have you figured out?"

"All those times you shrank after you ate Granny's goulash. Don't tell her I said so, dude, but that stuff gives you major gas. And what do you do when you have gas?"

"Giccup!" we both said together. The lightbulb in my head was starting to turn on.

"You've got to try it," Pablo said. "Right now."

I ran to the kitchen. Lark was there pointing her mini-Webcam at an egg that was sitting on the refrigerator shelf.

"Move," I said, trying to shove her aside.

"Daniel, can't you see I'm filming this egg."

"Try sitting on it," I said. "Maybe you'll hatch a better idea."

"For your information," she said, "I'm going to post this on my video blog, as an illustration of my thoughts about round things."

"Well, here's a news flash for you, sis. That egg isn't round, it's egg shaped. And no offense, but so is your rump, which is in my way."

When I went to move her aside, she tried to grab me by the hair. Robin's a jock and she can usually nail me. But Lark is a poet (at least in her own mind) and, lucky for me, poets aren't known for their quick reflexes. She missed me by a mile.

I ducked and reached into the fridge to grab a slab of Italian salami that Grandma Lola serves on

Italian night, along with this black pasta in squid ink she makes. (You won't believe this, but it's actually pretty tasty.) I bit off a hunk of the salami, jamming it in my mouth and swallowing it down, hardly chewing.

"Your eating habits are extremely repulsive," Lark said.

"Like I actually know what repulsive means," I answered.

"It means disgusting, foul, stomach-turning."

"Why didn't you just say so?" I didn't have time for a vocab lesson.

I bolted from the kitchen into the bathroom, stuck my face under the faucet, and gulped down about ten mouthfuls of water. When I came up for air, I already felt a giccup coming on.

I raced back to my room, slammed the door, and stood in front of Pablo.

"Here goes," I said to him.

Opening my mouth, I sucked in some more air, swallowed, then let one rip.

G-I-C-C-U-P!

I swear, you could have heard it all the way from Venice, California, to Tokyo, Japan, to Neptune and back again. It was loud and watery and long . . . or as Lark would say, totally *repulsive*.

We waited, the Pabs and I, for something to happen. My bedroom was quiet, except for our hamster, Brittany, who was exercising on the squeaky wheel in her cage. I don't know why she bothers to exercise. She's the fattest hamster in the universe. Goldie is always feeding her graham crackers with marshmallow sauce. That combo will pack on the pounds.

"Feel anything, dude?" Pablo asked.

I shook my head. But not for long.

Because before you could say "Brittany the Fat Hamster," my eyeballs were growling, my nostrils were blowing bubbles, my fingers were buzzing, and my knees were whistling.

As I shrank down, down, down to the size of the fourth toe on my left foot, all I could hear was Pablo shouting in the background.

"It's the giccups, stupid. It was always the giccups!"

CHAPTER 4

The Funkster's Funky Fact #4: Men get
hiccups more often than women.

I wanted to go and tell Great Granny Nanny right away. It was simple. Giccuping makes me shrink. This was the scientific discovery of a lifetime, better than when Thomas Edison invented the lightbulb. Okay, maybe not better, but at least as good. Okay, maybe not as good, but still, way up there.

Pablo refused to leave my room, though. He wanted a chance to win another gold medal in The Mini Man Olympics before we set out to find Granny Nanny.

"Dude," he said, "the Pablo has a chance to set a world record. This is no time for GUP interference."

By the way, GUP stands for Grown-Up People in Pablo speak. Personally, I don't consider Great Granny Nanny a GUP, because even though she's over eighty years old, she's as much fun as a kid— she's just stuck in a grown-up's body. But Pablo was already setting up for the next event, which was eraser lifting. He was trying to clean and jerk two large pink erasers.

Which he did, by the way.

He beat me hands down. I could barely get one eraser over my head. When I tried to lift two, I collapsed into a pathetic miniheap.

Eraser lifting was so much fun that our scientific discovery took a major backseat and we moved right on to the next event. And that was so much fun, we moved on to the next event. And the next. We actually forgot all about telling Granny Nanny our discovery.

I bet we spent an hour doing the other Mini Man Olympic events Pablo had dreamed up. Here's a tip: If you ever find yourself the size of a toe and you're stuck for something to do, participate in an Olympic competition on top of your desk. It's a blast.

We tossed the discus using plastic bottle caps from my mom's favorite sparkling pomegranate-flavored soda water. We did the high jump over a bar Pablo made out of a toothpick. We pole-vaulted over my stapler. Then we moved onto high dives, using my desk as a platform and Stinky Sock Mountain as our landing pool. I did a single back flip with a twist, but Pablo went for the highest degree of difficulty with a reverse three-and-a-half somersault. He nailed the landing when he sailed head first into a slightly smelly white tube sock.

As our final event, we ran a marathon around the

entire Underpants Valley, which had gotten pretty big since it contained about a week's worth of already-been-worn underwear. The finish line was at the foot of my La-Z-Boy chair.

Pablo beat me by a pair of boxer briefs.

All in all, he won six gold medals and I won . . . let me count . . . uh . . . that would be zero. I wasn't upset, though. I was just so glad to have a brother after all these years of not having one, I didn't mind if he won. Besides, he gave me a silver medal for every event I entered. He made them himself out of little bits of tinfoil and pieces of key chain.

We had just flopped down at the base of Stinky Sock Mountain for a rest when there was a knock at the door. Goldie stuck her head in.

"Daniel!" she yelled. "Mom says you have to come set the table for dinner."

I knew there was no danger of being discovered. When you're an inch tall, it's amazing how invisible you are. People just look right past you.

"Mom!" Goldie yelled. "Daniel's not in his room and it's his turn to set the table. It says so right there on the Chore Chart in the kitchen, so don't ask me to do it for him."

She slammed the door and left. I ask you, would it kill her to set the table for me? It's no big deal. You toss out a bunch of plates, scatter a little silverware around, and presto, you're done. My sisters actually have every chore in the house listed on their Chore Chart, and check off whose turn it is to do what on which day of the week. If you ask me, and I know you didn't, I think it's just an excuse for them to use their stupid fruit-scented markers and put their stupid fancy pineapple-smelling artwork up on the refrigerator.

My mom stuck her head in my room.

"Daniel!" she called. When I didn't answer, I could hear her mutter, "Where is that boy?" as she slammed the door shut.

A minute later the door opened again. Man, it was like a train station in there. This time it was Great Granny Nanny. She came all the way in and shut the door.

"I know you're in here, hotshots," she whispered. "Show yourselves."

Pablo and I came out from behind a black slithery sock I had to wear to brunch with my Aunt Janet last weekend. Granny got down on her hands and knees so she could see and hear us.

"Daniel, you're wanted for table-setting duty," she said. "You've got to come when you're called or you'll make everyone suspicious and that's not—"

Suddenly, she stopped talking.

"Wait a minute," she said, slapping her forehead with the palm of her hand. "You're little. When did you shrink? I didn't give you any goulash."

"Granny," I said to her, "we have some really exciting news to tell you. We have discovered the secret of how to make me shrink."

"It's the fish eggs, isn't it?" she said. "Yup, I knew it!"

"No, it's not the fish eggs."

"Then it's the seaweed-carrot combo, with ginger. My grandma always said ginger had powerful magic in it."

"It's not any food at all, Granny Nanny."

"It's what happens after the meal," Pablo said to her.

"Dessert?" Granny asked. "Dessert makes you shrink?"

"No, it's the giccups," Pablo and I both said at once, not able to hold the news in any longer.

Granny didn't believe us, so I had to demonstrate. Pablo tickled my nose by dangling one of my baseball socks over it. A chunk of dried mud from that ditch along the first-base line fell off my sock and thwonked me on the head. Wow, that hurt. Anyway, the old sock dangle worked and I sneezed my face off. Right then and there, I shot up to my normal size, which is about the same height as Great Granny Nanny.

"Okay, now watch this," I said to her.

I reached over to my desk and took a swig from a can of Coke that had been sitting there since the weekend. (Don't tell my mom. I'm not supposed to have food in my room.) It was flat and warm, but it did the trick. I swallowed some air, opened my mouth, and out came a slightly wet, slightly weak giccup. Not my strongest one, I'll admit, but still, technically, a giccup.

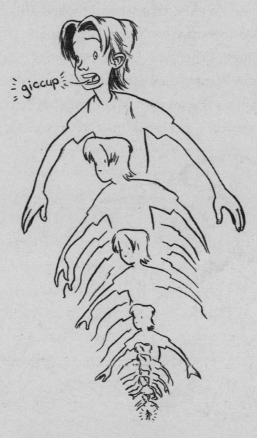

Within a second, my body went into its usual eyeball-growling, finger-buzzing, nose-bubbling, knee-whistling routine. And suddenly, bamo-slamo, down I went—until I was standing at the base of Stinky Sock Mountain, eye to eye with The Pablo.

I thought Granny was going to faint.

"Daniel!" she said. "This is powerful. Do you know what this means?"

She got up very close and looked us both in the eye. She was so close that when I looked at her face, I could see the wrinkles inside her wrinkles. I didn't mind, though. When you love someone as much as I love Granny Nanny, they can have more wrinkles than an elephant's ankle and you still think they're cool.

"This means," she said in a very serious tone,

"that you can shrink any time you want. It's within your power to control your size. Providing you have enough water or carbonated beverages around, in case you can't produce a giccup on your own."

She was right. The importance of the giccup discovery was just starting to sink in. It meant I could make myself little and return to my normal size whenever I wanted. This *was* an awesome power. A little scary, for sure. But also extremely cool.

Pablo was totally hyped up. He was already spinning out ideas a mile a minute.

"Listen up, bro," he said, talking even faster than usual. "We've got to make a list of all the most fun things we can do when you shrink. Because now, dude, we can do those things any time we want."

He was right. There was nothing stopping us now.

"We'll start tomorrow," he said, throwing his arm over my shoulder. "I know what's first on my list. Hot fudge sundae snowboarding. We'll make a mountain out of chocolate chip ice cream, scale it to the summit, and snowboard down. What's first on your list?"

"Whoa, there, Pabs. Tomorrow I have school."

"School? No biggie, bro. Just skip it."

"Pablo, I can't just skip school."

"Dude! Bro! Dan the Man! Tell me you didn't say what you just said."

"Well, it's the truth. What will I tell Mom? That I'm just not in the mood to go? Like that's going to be okay with her."

For the first time since I had met him, Pablo looked sad. Usually he's all full of energy and laughing and strutting. But now, he threw himself onto my black sock and cast his eyes downward. It was like looking at myself after I pitched a really terrible game. Like that one against the Red Sox when I let in thirty-four runs.

"Sounds to me," he said, "like maybe you don't want to spend the day with The Pablo. Maybe you'd rather hang out with your school pals."

"No, Pablo. That's not it."

"Fine. Hang out with your school friends. You just go ahead and do your thing, chicken wing."

"Pablo, you're not listening."

"You can tell me the truth," he went on, "because I'm okay by myself. I can find plenty of stuff to do. I've done it for ten years."

Granny put her finger out and patted Pablo on the head.

"There, there, honey," she said.

"Pablo," I said. "Listen up. I've been wanting a brother all my life. There's no one I'd rather be with than you."

"Honest, D. Funk?"

"Honest, P. Funk."

"So that means we can make our list and get going tomorrow?"

"Sure." I sighed. "I'll find a way." He was irresistible, that Pablo.

He jumped up and gave me a big smile. I'm kind of embarrassed to tell you what happened next, because I don't want to get all soppy or anything. But the truth is the truth.

I threw my arms around Pablo, and he threw his arms around me, and we had the best dude hug two brothers ever had.

CHAPTER 5

The Funkster's Funky Fact #5: The strongest muscle in the human body is the tongue.

I could hear my mom calling my name all over the house.

"I'd better go," I said to Pablo, breaking up our hug. "I have a table to set."

"I feel your pain, bro," Pablo said. "I'll be here working on our list. You got any Post-it Notes?"

"There, on the desk." Granny lifted him up and carried him over to my desk.

"See you soon, Pabs," I said.

"Hasta, pasta."

As he spoke, he didn't even look up. He was already pulling a Post-it Note off the pad on my desk. It wasn't easy for him. The note was bigger than he was, and he kept stepping on the sticky part and getting his feet stuck.

I asked Granny to tickle my nose with a feather from my pillow. Then I sneezed and popped back up to myself. I rubbed my eyes as I walked out of my room. I had been doing a lot of shrinking and popping back up that day. The old bod was starting to feel it.

I headed down the hall toward the dining room, which isn't really a dining room but part of the living room where we eat.

"Where have you been?" Goldie shouted as I passed her room.

"I shrunk down to the size of a toe and disappeared," I said.

"Very funny, Daniel. What a lame excuse for getting out of your chores."

Life is weird. You tell the truth, and nobody believes you.

Our house is this big old wooden bungalow on the canals in Venice, and like most of the houses around us, it's laid out in an unusual way. People who live on the canals, which are these little waterways with ducks paddling around in them, don't mind their houses being odd. It's a known fact that folks who like to step over duck poop to get to their garages also like to have strange houses.

Our house is unusual because it has a ton of rooms, but they don't follow any logical order. They ramble on and on like a train. For instance, Great Granny Nanny lives in the sun porch at the back of the house. And my grandma Lola has a triangle-shaped room in back of hers. My mom, who's a vet, takes care of animals in her office, which is in a cottage way out in the backyard. Goldie's room is made from a former closet and has a ladder leading to Robin and Lark's room, which used to be part of mine.

You probably noticed that all the rooms I've mentioned are occupied by people of the womanly variety. Except for me and now Pablo, there isn't a guy in our house. Even Bruce, our new parakeet, who I bought last week specifically because he was supposed to be a male, laid an egg the other day. Now my sisters have adopted him and changed his name to Sweetie Tweetie.

Way to go, Bruce.

Anyway, nothing in our house is where you'd expect it to be, even the dining room. It's just a big table at the end of the living room. But it is where we eat, so that's where I headed to set the table. By the time I got there, my mom was already doing it for me.

"I'll finish that, Mom," I said, taking the last fork and laying it down next to the last plate.

"Sure you're up for it, champ?" Robin said. "You don't want to exhaust yourself."

My mom just laughed and walked into the kitchen. Robin was sitting on a chair, writing in a book with a (you guessed it) pink pen that had a fluffy pink pom-pom on the end. It was the girliest pen you've ever seen, but since I'm basically a nice guy, I decided to cut her a break and not mention the ridiculous fluffy furry pinky thing going on at the tip.

"What's up, Robs? Taking notes on what you're going to wear tomorrow?"

"Actually, I am," Robin said. "I've started a new hobby. I'm keeping a fashion diary."

"You're kidding me, right? I thought I was joking."

"Why would anyone joke about a fashion journal, Daniel? There's nothing funny about it."

"Except everything."

"That shows what you know, Mister I-wear-the-same-T-shirt-every-day."

"Robin, what could anyone possibly write in a fashion journal?"

"Well, every day I'm going to write down all my ideas for cute outfits. And in the morning, I'll read them over and decide which one to wear."

Okay, friends, welcome to my world. As a member of the Funk House of Women, this is the kind of nightmare I have to deal with all the time. It's bad enough to have a sister who takes videos of eggs sitting in the refrigerator. Or another one who cries when her Barbie is having a bad hair day. But now I had one who had actually gone out and purchased a hot pink patent-leather journal to write down her cute ideas for outfits. She'd used money that could have gone for something normal, like a catcher's mitt or sour Gummy Bears or new skateboard wheels.

And please, can someone tell me . . . why would anyone spend a nanosecond writing down what they might want to wear the next day? What happened to rolling out of bed, picking up whatever is lying on the floor, putting it on, and going out the door? Isn't that the way a person is supposed to get dressed?

It's the natural way. You don't see lions in the jungle styling their manes with a blow-dryer. Or zebras deciding if they should wear the stripes or the polka dots. Or parrots wondering if the red feather clashes with the blue feather. No, I say human beings are like the other animals. We were meant to look the way we look, until girls came along and invented fashion do's and don'ts. Who said that you have to wear underpants every day? Or that both your shoes have to match? Or that you can't wear black knee socks with shorts?

Girls, that's who. Girls like my sister Robin.

"Let me have that book," I said to Robin. I had to see with my own two eyes that someone in my same gene pool was actually keeping this lamest of diaries.

"No way!" Robin screamed, clutching the journal to her pink polka-dot sweatshirt. "It's highly personal."

"Come on, Robs. I'll only make fun of you a little tiny bit."

"I'd rather be seen in Lark's old flip-flops than have your paws flipping through my private fashion thoughts," she said.

And then she took a little gold key off a chain

around her neck and put it into a little gold lock on the diary's front cover.

"You're kidding me, right? You're actually putting that book under lock and key?"

"I don't want you snooping, Daniel."

"Okay," I said, heaving a giant sigh. "I'll just have to survive without knowing what you're thinking about wearing to school tomorrow. It'll be tough, but I can do it. I'm a survivor, you know."

Robin lunged for me, but before she had time to grab me and give me an Egyptian rug burn (which she's expert at), my Mom and Lola and Granny came in with dinner. It was Lola's night to cook, which always means that we're having something from another country. A global dinner, she calls it. Sometimes her global recipes can get pretty weird, like the night she made fried duck feet from China. But tonight she had pulled off a pretty decent-sounding meal.

"Who wants chicken and vegetable curry?" she called. "It's from a recipe I picked up in an ashram outside of Mumbai."

Before any of the sisters could get to the table, I dug into the serving bowl and heaped a big mound of rice and curry onto my plate. I happen to have a bigger appetite than my sisters, who are not only named after birds, but eat like them too.

Lark came out of her room carrying her mini Webcam. She focused it on my plate as I took my first bite.

"Lark Sparrow Funk, put that thing down," my mom said. "There is nothing to shoot here."

"I am recording the repulsive eating habits of the American preteen male," Lark said, zooming in on my face.

"Excellent," I said. "Then record this."

I opened my mouth really wide so she'd get a good close-up of all the half-chewed food. When she saw the muck inside my mouth, Lark actually screamed and dropped her camera in the curry bowl.

I laughed so hard I almost spit my rice all over the table. Fortunately, I have excellent tongue control and managed to catch most of the rice before it spewed all over her.

"I don't know why you have to record everything you see, Larkie," Lola said.

"Yeah," agreed Granny. "It's much more fun to put a rose between your teeth and dance the rumba. That's what I did when I was a girl."

What'd I tell you about Granny Nanny? How many kids do you know whose great-grandma danced around with a rose in her teeth?

I took another bite of Lola's curry.

"This is delicious, Lola," I said. Suddenly, I chomped down on something red and hot and spicy. Holy macaroni! It was the hottest chili pepper I had ever tasted. My mouth felt like it was shooting flames into the air!

I reached for a glass of water to put out the fire and gulped it down. The water went flooding into my stomach, where it turned into a tsunami.

My stomach started hopping around like the Easter bunny. Water was still rolling around in the back of my throat.

Oh yeah. I bet you're thinking that you know what was about to happen.

And you're right.

I giccuped. Right there at the dinner table.

It was a long, rolling, chili-fired giccup.

I think we all know what happened next.

CHAPTER 6

The Funkster's Funky Fact #6: The only sport that
has been played on the moon is golf.

Let me put it this way.

One minute I was *at* the dinner table.

The next minute I was *under* it.

Faster than you can say "ashram in Mumbai," I shrunk to my mini size, slid off the edge of the chair, flew under the table, and landed flat on my hindquarters. Staring at me as I landed was Princess, our slobbery bulldog, who always sits under the table when we eat, hoping to catch any falling scraps.

I don't even want to go into the fact that our bulldog is named Princess. I think by now you know how that happened. Don't blame me. I voted for Duke.

Princess came over and sniffed me so hard, I thought I was going to be sucked up into bulldog nostril heaven. She was growling.

"It's just me, Princess. A mini me, but me."

When she heard my voice, which she could do easily because dogs have such good hearing, Princess cocked her head to one side and started to whine.

"Sshh, Princess," I whispered. "Nix the whining."

I didn't want everyone looking under the dinner table to check out why Princess was whining. Then they'd find me there. Come to think of it, I wondered how Granny was explaining my absence up above.

Poor Granny. This was probably very stressful for

her. I had to get busy and get her out of this jam. I knew what I had to do.

I plopped down flat on the rug and rubbed my whole face in it. Lucky for me, we have a dog that sheds and a vacuum cleaner that doesn't work. There was enough dog hair in that rug to make the entire population of China sneeze themselves into outer space.

I took a deep breath and waited. It took exactly half a second.

"Ah choo," I went. That was followed by about six more where that came from.

"Ah choo! Ah choo! Ah choo! Ah choo! Ah choo! Ah chooooo!"

Thump! What was that?

Oh, it was my head thumping on the underside of the tabletop as I instantly sprouted up, back to my regular size.

Oww! That hurt!

"Okay, brainless, what are you doing under there?" said my sister Robin.

"Whining like a dog," I answered, trying to prevent everyone from noticing that I had just shrunk down to the size of a toe.

"Daniel, you're so funny," Goldie said. "You make me laugh."

"Goldie, there is nothing funny about an adolescent

boy falling off his chair and whining like a dog under the table," Lark said. "If you want real humor, read my poem called '*My Ticklish Wicklish Self.*' It's on my blog."

"Would that be www.my-poetry-sucks.com?" I crawled out from under the table and got back on my chair. It was amazing to me that I could totally shrink and disappear under the table, and no one except Granny Nanny was aware of what had happened, not even my mom. I guess most moms don't go around assuming their sons have the ability to shrink.

"Are you okay, honey?" my mom asked, rubbing my head where I had bumped it.

"He's fine," said Robin. "That's what he gets for clowning around at the dinner table."

"I think he may have gotten a little dizzy there for a second," Granny Nanny said, "and that's why he fell."

"I wasn't dizzy," I said. Granny Nanny flashed me a look that said, *Go with me here, Daniel. I've got a plan.*

"I mean, *at first* I wasn't dizzy," I said quickly. "Then I got extremely dizzy."

Granny nodded at me in approval.

"I hope you're not getting sick," Lola said. "I can make you some dried licorice root tea with green onions. The Chinese say it prevents colds and flu."

"No thanks, Lola," I said. "The fried duck feet

sort of turned me off Chinese cooking for a while."

"I don't blame you," she said with a laugh. "I found them a little chewy myself."

My mom reached out and touched my forehead.

"Let's just keep an eye on you," she said.

"If he's not feeling well in the morning, I'll stay home with him," Granny chimed in.

I could see the wheels turning in her brain. She was getting me my day with Pablo, slowly but surely. *You rock, Great Granny Nanny.*

"I'd hate to miss school," I said, "but maybe I should rest up tomorrow. The rocket launch is Saturday and I don't want to miss that."

"That will certainly be a very special day for my budding scientist here," my mom said, giving me a proud smile. She was hoping that one of us would become a vet, like her, so whenever science was involved, she turned all mushy.

"Hey, I'm launching a rocket too," Robin said, inserting herself into the conversation as always. "And mine is way cuter than his."

"It's not a fashion show, Robs. It's a scientific endeavor."

"I bet if those astronauts had gone to the moon in a really hot looking rocket, we would have made it all the way there," she said.

"Uh . . . news flash, Robs. We did make it all the way there."

"I knew that," she said. "I was just testing to see if you did."

"For your information, I'm going to the launch too," Lark said. "Ms. Addison has asked me to cover it for the upper school newspaper. I'm going to blog about it from the point of view of the rocket. What it feels. What it thinks."

I swear, my sister Lark is totally nuts. What could a rocket think? I'm going to go up in the air. Then I'm going to come down. And I hope I don't crash in between. The end.

"Daniel," my mom said, "if you're still feeling woozy, maybe you should go rest in your room."

"I'll bring your dinner in there," Granny said.

"And I'll bring you tea," Lola added.

I tried to look weak as I got up from the table and headed for my room.

Man, this was working out really well. A day off from school. A list of fun things to do.

And now, room service.

What could be better?

CHAPTER 7

The Funkster's Funky Fact #7: The average pencil can be sharpened 17 times and draw a line 35 miles long before it runs out of lead.

Pablo was writing like a madman when I walked back into the bedroom. Oh, he doesn't write with a whole pencil. Granny has made him a box of pencil tips that she sharpens for him every day. She likes him to practice his penmanship. A couple of years ago, she taught him how to print, and now she's teaching him cursive. She checks his work over every day with a magnifying glass because she says that being little is no excuse for having poor penmanship.

"What's up, pup?" Pablo said, stopping his writing just long enough to pick up the PabloPhone.

"Chicken curry," I said. "You didn't miss much."

Pablo put down the phone and continued to write at top speed. I noticed that his tongue was sticking out between his front teeth, just like mine does when I write. None of the sisters do that. I wondered if that was a particular habit of the Funk men. Maybe our dad stuck his tongue out when he wrote, too. I wish I could remember. I remember his big hands with a silver snake ring on one finger and a freckle on his palm shaped like a bear paw. And I remember his hat with a white eagle feather in it. I don't know what Pablo remembers, because we've never talked about our dad. It would be too sad.

"Here," Pablo said into the PabloPhone, pushing the yellow Post-it Note over to me. "I've made a list of the five most fun things to do when you shrink. Read what's on it."

I glanced down at the paper. It was mostly empty, with a tiny bit of scribble-scrabble in the middle.

"I can't read this, Pabs. It looks like a flea wrote it."

"First off, bro, let me say that comparing The

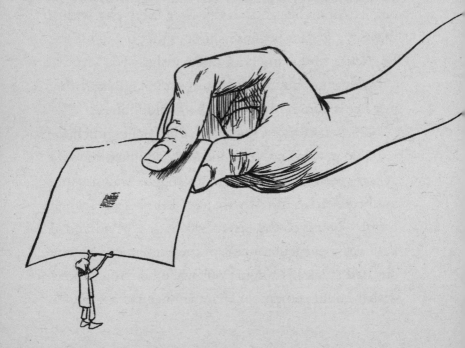

Pablo to a flea is very offensive. I am not an insect, and I do not bite."

"Sorry, Pablo. I didn't mean to hurt your feelings."

"I forgive you," he said, and I believe he did. "Second of all, let me point out that my writing will look just fine if you come down to my size."

You can do that, Daniel Funk. You can do that any old time you want.

"Don't mind if I do," I said.

I sat on the edge of my desk and took a swig of the Coke. In about ten seconds, it produced just the giccup I needed. For the fourth time that day, my eyeballs started to growl, my nostrils bubbled, and my fingers buzzed. Just as my knees began to do their whistling thing, I looked across my room and noticed that Brittany was flashing me a weird look from inside her cage.

"Bet you can't do this, hamster lady," I said.

The next thing I knew, I was as small as Pablo. I knew that for two reasons. First, the can of Coke sitting next to me on the desk was as tall as a twenty-story building. And second, Brittany was suddenly as big as a polar bear. Her fluffy white cheeks were huge and her whiskers seemed to stretch out forever. She continued to stare at me, and I wondered what she was thinking. Could it be *Wow, that Daniel is doing a heck of a lot of shrinking today.* Or maybe she was just having regular rodent thoughts like *I think I'll shred up some newspaper and make a poop in my cage.*

Right away, Pablo was in my face, shoving the Post-it Note in front of me.

"I've given the matter a lot of thought," he said, "and here they are. My top five most fun things to do when in a miniature state."

I looked at the list. It said, "Pablo's Perfect Phive."

"That's not how you spell five," I said to him.

"It's the way I spell it," he said. "I like my words to start with P, because Pablo starts with a P, which makes it my favorite letter of the alphabet."

Why not, I thought. When you don't have to take spelling tests, you can spell any old way you want.

I read over the list. It was total Pablo, all the way. If you read it, you'd think you were reading the program guide for the extreme sports network. In fact, here it is. Read it over and let me know if you agree.

PABLO'S PERFECT PHIVE: TOP FUN THINGS TO DO LIST
Snowboard down a hot fudge sundae
Surf big waves in the bathtub
Go trampolining on a marshmallow
Get sling-shot out of one of the sisters' scrunchies
Daniel's choice

LIN OLIVER

You have to say this for my brother, Pablo. He totally knows what fun is.

"Okay," he said, the second I finished reading. "I've left the last one blank for you. Now you add something and we'll have our perfect day."

"I can't come up with anything nearly as fun as these," I said.

"Sure you can. Just use your imagination."

I thought and thought.

"Okay," I said at last. "How about diving into a sugar bowl?"

"I'm not feeling it, bro. Diving into a sugar bowl is fun because why?"

"Well, when you get out, you get to lick the sugar off your fingers."

"Dude, dude, dude," Pablo said, shaking his head and patting me on the back. "My poor, sorry, fun-deprived little dude. The Pablo has so much to teach you."

Pablo frowned, and I noticed that when he did, he got little wrinkles in his forehead just like I do. Whenever my mom sees them, she always touches my forehead and smoothes them away.

I didn't like feeling like I was a total zip in the fun department. So I got serious, scratched my head, looked around the room, and came up with the first thing I saw.

"How about this?" I said. "Let's invade Brittany's cage and take a run on her exercise wheel."

"Negatory," Pablo said. "We do not go into hamster cages because hamsters poop in there. That simple fact makes it a big fat NO in my book. And I'm not even getting into the aroma issue."

Boy, was I feeling like a doofus. Suddenly, every fun thing I had ever done left my head and all that remained in there was homework assignments, phone numbers, and baseball stats.

"Let me help you out here," Pablo said. "Fun is everywhere. Just look around. What do you see?"

I glanced around my room. I saw the Creature Condo Corner, where we keep some of our pets. But Pablo had already rejected the Brittany idea, so I didn't dare suggest anything to do with the pets. I looked in the other direction and saw my red Porsche poster hanging on the wall. Big deal, you couldn't actually take a poster for a drive. I looked up and saw the old wooden fan on the ceiling.

Wait! The fan! There was an idea.

"We could hang on the ceiling fan and fly," I suggested.

"Now you're thinking," Pablo said. "The Pablo does love the idea of flying."

It's amazing how alike we are. I love the idea of

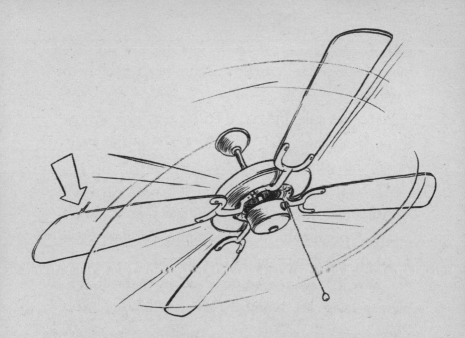

flying too. In fact, I've always wanted to fly. When I was really little, I used to dream that I was a bird flying over the city to my nest. When I'd wake up and have breakfast, I'd pretend that my cereal was a bowl of worms that my mommy bird had brought me.

Okay, I'm sorry I told you that. It's pretty embarrassing. If you could see me now, you'd see that my face is really red. So let's make a deal. Forget I ever said that, okay? Unless you want to drop me a note and let me in on an embarrassing thought you had when you were a little kid. Then we'd be even.

"Not to discourage the flying thing or anything," Pablo said, "but there is one small problem with your plan. When we turn on the fan, it's going to stir up a major breeze, and miniguys like us won't be able to hang on."

Point well taken. Maybe I'd have to give up the flying idea. Then, suddenly, the old Funkster brain kicked into gear. I had an idea.

If you ask me, and I know you didn't, it wasn't just a regular idea, either. It was a brilliant idea. An inspiration. A brainstorm. A head-spinner. In fact, it was so good, I couldn't even say it out loud.

"I have it!" I whispered. "The activity that will complete our wish list. Number Phive on Pablo's Perfect Phive."

"Well, lay it on me, bro. The Pablo is dying to hear."

I leaned over and whispered it into Pablo's ear.

I am proud to say that my idea stopped him dead in his tracks. Yup, him. Pablo Picasso Diego Funk. The king of fun. The emperor of excitement. The brainiac of buzz.

I had come up with an idea that had blown away even him.

CHAPTER 8

The Funkster's Funky Fact #8: If you shouted in outer space, even if someone were right next to you, they wouldn't be able to hear you.

Don't pretend you don't want to know what I told Pablo.

We both know that you do. It's a known fact that when one person whispers something in another person's ear, everyone has to know what it is, even if they didn't care one tiny little bit in the first place. Secrets are like that.

And since I'm your pal, I'm not going to make you wait any longer.

Here it is.

Remember my Science Club? And remember the model rockets that we were building? And remember the launch in La Brea Park? And remember what day that launch was?

That's right. Give yourself an A on the Funkster Quiz. It *was* Saturday. Two days away.

And here's what I told Pablo. That on Saturday, we would go to La Brea Park, tuck ourselves into a model rocket, and do what model rockets do best.

Blast off into space.

If that wasn't the perfect end to Pablo's Perfect Phive, then my name isn't Daniel Eagle Funk.

And I have a birth certificate to prove that it is.

CHAPTER 9

I was still pretty dizzy the next morning.

Don't worry, I wasn't *actually* dizzy. But I told my mom I was so she'd let me stay home from school. Pablo and I had the perfect day planned, and I wasn't about to let a little thing like school stand in the way.

It worked out just right because that day my mom was seeing cats at the Venice Animal Clinic Cats Only Day and not in her office at home. That meant that Pablo and I had the run of the place. Along with Great Granny Nanny.

"Bye, Daniel. I hope you feel better," Goldie said as she walked out the front door.

"Like he's really sick," Robin said under her breath, following Goldie out and letting the screen door slam in my face.

"Don't touch my lap harp," called Lark, as if I had been dying to go into her room and strum the stupidest instrument ever invented. Sometimes she walks around playing that thing while she recites one of her poems, and I'm telling you, the combo makes you want to run to Alaska, bury your head in a glacier, and never come out.

Wait. I don't think you can bury your head in a glacier. Anyway, you get the idea.

"Get some rest, honey," my mom said, grabbing her vet bag with her stethoscope and stuff in it. She has stickers of birds all over it because she's such a bird nut. For Christmas, I made her a sticker of the red-naped sapsucker that I traced from one of her bird guidebooks. She got all teary and said it was the best Christmas present she ever got. My dad was a bird lover too, and I think it made her think of him.

"Don't forget to eat some raw garlic," Lola said to me. "It's excellent for the immune system."

"And for bad breath," I added.

"Don't be narrow-minded, dear. In many cultures, people enjoy the smell of bad breath."

"Remind me not to visit those cultures," I called after her as she headed to the car, dragging a large hand-beaded Indonesian baby carrier on her back. She couldn't wait to show it to her sixth-period World Culture class. The strange thing is, I bet they couldn't wait to see it either. Lola is that kind of teacher. You know, the weird one that at first you make fun of, but then wind up loving more than all your other teachers. Some of her ex-students have even built sweat lodges in their backyards because of her.

Finally, the parade of exiting Funk females ended, and we could get started. The Pabs and I had a wish list of things to accomplish, and I couldn't wait to check off each activity.

I went to my room, where Granny was trying to wake Pablo up. He was asleep in the little Native American teepee she had made for him out of twigs and an old pair of moccasins I had worn in kindergarten. My sisters think it's weird that I've developed this sudden interest in having Granny's miniature sculptures on my bed table. What they don't know is that they are Pablo's houses.

"He's saying he needs his beauty rest," Granny said when I walked in. "He won't get up."

I put the magnifying glass up to the flap of the teepee and looked in. There was Pablo, asleep in the curve of a dried eucalyptus leaf.

"Anyone ready for Brother Bonding Day?" I said.

Pablo threw his little blanket, which Granny had made out of a piece of satin from my baby blanket, over his head.

"The Pablo needs his rest," he said. "Brother bonding can wait."

"I have here Pablo's Perfect Phive," I said, dangling the Post-it Note in front of the flap. "My goal is to check off the first four today, and top it all off with number five tomorrow. But I guess that's not what you had in mind."

In a flash, Pablo bolted upright, sprang to his feet, and pulled on the shirt that was lying next to his bed. No fashion diaries for the Funk men!

"I'm ready," he said. "What's first?"

"First, I have to shrink."

"Well do your stuff, Mister Tuff," he said. "What are you waiting for?"

I carried him into the kitchen, and Granny made us some breakfast. One Cheerio for Pablo, and a bowl of oatmeal for me. When we had finished, I took a swig of my mom's pomegranate-flavored soda water. I felt it bubbling in the back of my throat.

Happily, I opened my mouth and waited for the giccup to come out. As I waited, I looked down at the Post-it Note with our list on it. This could be the best day of my life so far, I thought to myself. And it was all thanks to Pablo's Perfect, Phantastic, Phabulous, Phenomenal Phive.

"I love you, little Post-it Note," I whispered. I looked around to make sure no one had heard me. And then I shrunk.

Woo hoo, world! It's me, Daniel Funk. Ready for action. I say bring on the fun!

CHAPTER 10

The Funkster's Funky Fact #10: The average human body has enough fat to produce seven bars of soap.

Okay, guys. Here's a tip.

If you're ever the size of a toe and want to have the most amazing day of your life, come on over to my house at 344 Pacific Lane and hang out with me and Pablo. You won't be sorry.

I'm not going to lie to you. We had more fun that day than I've had on any single day of my life. I can't even tell you all the details because if I did, you'd put this book down immediately and start working on figuring out ways to shrink yourself. That's how great it was.

But I will give you a few highlights because I'm a sharing and caring kind of guy.

We decided not to start with the first item on our Pablo's Perfect Phive, which was snowboarding down a hot fudge sundae because we had just had breakfast and wanted to save that for when we were hungry and really in the mood to do a face plant in a bowl of chocolate chip ice cream. Instead, we kicked off the day with marshmallow trampolining.

Granny, who was as excited about this day as we were, stacked a bunch of marshmallows into a pyramid on the kitchen floor. First we jumped on the top one and did flips and somersaults and twists. Then we bounced like maniacs all the way down to the bottom. We trampolined so much, the marshmallows started turning to goo under our feet.

While we were bouncing, Granny got her sculpting tools out and made us surfboards out of soap. They worked great too. Not only did they float, but they went really fast through the water. We carved up those waves in the bathtub like real Hawaiian surfing champs. Granny kept the splashing going with her hands, which created some ten-footers for us to shoot the curl in. At least they seemed like ten-footers to us. They were probably only six inches high, but when you're an inch tall, that's still six times bigger than you are.

I wiped out pretty often, but Pablo had a natural gift for surfing. Except he's goofy footed, which I am not. (For you land-locked guys out there, that means he surfs with his right foot in front.) It was the first real difference I had noticed between us. Other than that, we are totally identical, even down to the crooked shape of our pinky fingers.

We surfed for a long time, until our surfboards

started to dissolve in the bathwater. I made a mental note that next time, Granny was going to have to come up with something other than soap to make our surfboards out of. Not to be wasteful, I did scrub my knees and elbows with what was left of my board.

Snowboarding was next. By that time, we were in the mood for some frozen refreshments.

I don't want to overload you with tips, but here's one more you've got to know. It's essential information. If you're ever snowboarding down a hot fudge sundae, remember that you have to snowboard *around* the cherry on top, because if you use it as a mogul and try to jump off it, you'll wipe out in the whipped cream for sure.

You'll thank me for this one day. I know it.

Wiping out in the whipped cream does have its advantages, though. You get to eat it.

Before moving on to the next item on the list, we had to take a little while to recover from all the ice cream we had stuffed into our bodies. When you're the size of a toe, two chocolate chips can send your stomach into overload. While we were digesting, we took the pencil point and checked off the first three items on Pablo's Perfect Phive.

"We have to make another list right away," I said to Pablo.

"What's wrong with this one?"

"It's too short. We're more than halfway through it."

"You're definitely getting the hang of this fun thing," Pablo said with a laugh. "I promise—as soon as we finish this list, we'll make another one. Deal, D. Funk?"

"Deal, P. Funk!"

We high-fived and hooted like a couple of toe-sized idiots.

The next two events were certain to be the most exciting. The human sling shot. I mean, how great does that sound? And going up in a model rocket . . . friends, I think we can all agree that's a total *blast*.

Sorry for the little joke. I'll never do it again. I swear.

"You hotshots go get a scrunchy from the girls' room," Granny said. "I've got to clean up this fudgy mess you made in the kitchen."

We hopped into the Ken and Barbie four by four, which we'd been cruising around in all morning, and took off like Indy 500 drivers. We picked Lark and Robin's room for the scrunchy hunt, rather than Goldie's, because Robin's was the farthest from the kitchen, and that meant we could burn rubber all the way down the hall.

The scrunchies were on top of the dresser they share, and I'm here to tell you, the top was a long, long way up from where we were, on the floor.

"No problemo," Pablo said. "Are we or are we not world-class trampoliners?"

He jumped from the jeep, scaled the face of the bottom drawer where Lark keeps her sweaters, and climbed inside. Lark's stuff is on one side of the dresser and Robin's is on the other side. I could tell he was on Lark's side because all of Robin's sweaters are pink and all of Lark's are dark, depressing colors. Being a poet and all, my sister Lark never wears bright colors, because they might actually make her look good, which might make her happy, which might make her stop writing those depressing poems, which might actually make her fun to be around, and we all know, fun is definitely not Lark's thing.

If you ask me, and I know you didn't, I don't get why anyone would want to own so many dark-colored sweaters. I mean, what's the point? You could just wear the same one every day and none of your friends would know the difference. Unless they stood really close to you and breathed deeply around your armpit area, and who wants friends like that?

Once he was inside the drawer, Pablo started jumping up and down on Lark's sweaters. He jumped higher and higher until he got a really huge bounce going. Then, with a big "yeeeooowww," he leaped into the air, somersaulted, and bamo-slamo, landed smack in the middle of the next open drawer.

"Come on, bro. Jump with me! This is fun," he hollered.

I did. And it was.

We repeated the same thing with all three drawers—jumping and somersaulting from the sweaters to the socks, the socks to the underwear (we got out of there fast!) and finally up to last drawer that held Lark's

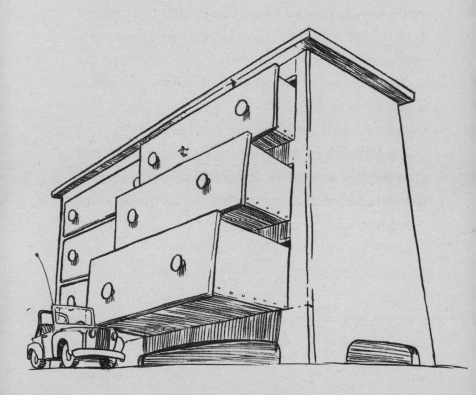

scarves, headbands, makeup, and other unidentified girly-type stuff. From there, it was an easy climb to the top, where the scrunchies were.

I grabbed for the first scrunchy I saw, but before I could start down, Pablo took hold of my arm.

"Dude, check out that book. It's the brightest pink I've ever seen. What kind of book could that be?"

I knew what it was. It was the journal. Robin's pink patent-leather fashion journal.

Right then and there, an idea came to me for something that would be really fun. It was my second great idea of the week. I know, I know, it wasn't on Pablo's Perfect Phive list. But it should have been. For sure.

"Hey Pablo," I whispered. "I've got something great for us to do."

"The Pablo is always up for fun," he said.

I told him all about Robin's journal. Then I told him my idea of what we should do with that journal. When he heard it, his eyes lit up like fireworks on the Fourth of July.

CHAPTER 11

The Funkster's Funky Fact #11: To find out how much you would weigh on the moon, take your weight and divide by six.

Okay, I have to admit something right here and now.

You will think my idea is fun only if you're someone who really likes to annoy your sisters or brothers. If you're the mature, I-get-along-perfectly-with-my-brothers-and-sisters type, then I'm warning you right now, you probably won't be amused by this. I confess, I'm pretty immature in the mature department. Sometimes it is extremely enjoyable for me to annoy my sisters. Especially Robin.

There, I've said it.

It's not like she doesn't deserve it. I mean, take the other night. I was sprawled on the couch watching the Lakers game, having a great old time, when she comes along and snags the remote control right out of my hand, and turns on one of her MTV dating shows. Yup, in the middle of a Lakers game!

"Hey," I said, grabbing for the remote. "Give that back."

"No," was all she answered.

Don't get me wrong. I'm all for watching your favorite shows on TV. I mean, give me a Wrestling Smackdown or anything with the word *gladiator* in the title, and I'm there. But dating shows? Come on, there are a million of those shows that she could watch at any other time—*Blind Date*, *Good Date*, *Bad Date*, *Next Date*, *Date Me!*, *Want a Date?* What's the difference? They all ask the same burning question: Is this guy cute or what?

I tried to explain to her, in what I thought was a very nice tone of voice, that basketball games are more important than dating shows. But she wouldn't fork over the remote and just sat there staring at her stupid show while I missed the end of the Lakers game. And friends, it was the play-offs. Enough said.

So when I saw her fashion journal sitting right there in front of me, I had a thought. What if we just flipped through the pages and left Robin a few choice notes with our comments? Sort of like my teacher Mr. Schrode does in the margins of my English papers.

It would drive Robin nuts to think that someone, namely me, had been poking around in her private fashion thoughts. Plus, I would get a chance to express to her some of my deepest thoughts about her new hobby. And hey, my input might even help her out, give her some new insights. On the other hand, it might simply annoy her.

Either way, it sounded like fun.

"Wow," said Pablo, when I explained my idea to him. "Wow. Wow. Wow. Daniel Funk, I am proud to call you my brother."

"So you like it?"

"Like it? It's buzzin', cuzzin."

I'm pretty sure that meant he liked it.

I walked across the top of the dresser to the pink diary and tried to open it up. Nothing doing.

"Oh, wait," I said to Pablo. "I forgot. She's got it all locked up with a key and everything."

"No problemo," Pablo said with a grin. "Advantage Number 34 of being small is that we are capable of crawling through keyholes."

Of course. For a minute there, I had forgotten that I was a mini-guy. Once you get used to being the size of a toe, you hardly even think about it.

"I'll go get the supplies," Pablo said. "You can do the safecracking."

"What supplies?" I asked.

"We'll need Post-it Notes," Pablo said. "In case there's not enough room for our comments.

With that, he held his nose and jumped feet first

off the dresser. He went down straight as a pencil and landed on the seat of the Ken and Barbie four by four. Don't try this at home, guys, because trust me, you'll get hurt. But when you're as little as we are, you are almost weightless, like astronauts on the moon. You can do amazing things and not get hurt.

Pablo went screeching off down the hall, and I stepped onto the top of the diary. Whoa, I felt like I was swimming in a sea of pink. I walked over to the lock, rolled myself up into a ball like a doodlebug and wedged myself into the keyhole.

Plop! I dropped down into darkness. Inside the lock, it was really hard to see, so I started grabbing at random things until I found a little lever that moved.

I pulled on it with all my might and heard a click.

Unrolling my body as much as I could, I was able to stick my head up out of the keyhole. I looked around and saw that the prongs on the lock were hanging loose from the patent leather strap. It had worked! The lock had snapped open, just like that. I tell you, it's good to be little.

By that time, Pablo had returned with the Post-it Notes.

"Watch out down there," I hollered. "Heavy load coming down."

I crawled out of the lock and leaned against the diary with all my weight, which couldn't have been more than a couple of ounces.

"Aaarrrggg," I grunted, throwing my itty-bitty body into the effort. Little by little, I pushed the diary to the edge of the dresser until it finally fell onto the floor. It landed with a thud and opened to a page that was covered with Robin's fancy handwriting. It was a messy mass of pink ink.

I pencil-jumped down from the dresser, just like Pablo did, and landed on my feet, right in the center of the page.

We got to reading right away. To my surprise, Pablo was a pretty good reader for a kid who had never gone to school. Granny Nanny taught him well. But it took us forever to read even one sentence. Our eyes had to travel all the way across the huge page. You don't think about this, but when you're the size of a toe, your eyes are the size of a mouse's tooth. Not that I've ever seen a mouse's tooth, but you get the idea.

We didn't have all day, so I decided to speed things up and unshrink myself. I made myself sneeze, which wasn't too hard. All I had to do was stick my face in the fluffy pink pom-pom at the end of Robin's stupid diary pen. In one second, I had popped up to my regular size. I scrunched down on the floor so that I could share the fun with Pablo, and read out loud from page one of Robin's journal.

"I'm thinking of combining green shorts with a purple tank top," I read. Pablo shoved the Post-it Note pad over to me.

I can't decide if this combo is really cute or really weird, Robin had written. Boy, that Robin had some heavy thoughts spinning around in that pea brain of hers. Who knew she was such a deep thinker?

"The girl wants the truth," Pablo said, "so the truth it is. Write *It's really really weird, just like you!*"

I wrote what he said and stuck the Post-it on the page.

"Let's hear more," Pablo said, cracking himself up. I read out loud from another journal entry.

Note to self, Robin had written. *Match purses with shoes. Red purse with red shoes. Brown purse with brown shoes. Black purse with black shoes. Green purse with—*

"Enough!" Pablo interrupted. "I can't take any more!"

I pulled off another Post-it Note and wrote this. *Note to self: Get a life!*

Pablo and I howled as I slapped the Post-it Note over that entry.

"Boys!" Granny Nanny called from the kitchen. "Bring the scrunchy in here now if you want to have time for the last event. Your mom will be home soon."

"We'd better stop," I said. "I still have to shrink back down."

"Just one more," Pablo begged. He pointed to a sentence that had a little picture next to it. "Here. Read this."

"Deep thought for the day," I read. "Why do shoes always come in pairs?" And next to this, Robin had drawn a big pink brain.

"Wow, that is deep," Pablo said. "I wonder what her shallow thoughts are."

We couldn't stop laughing. We thought we were the funniest guys on the planet.

Your deep thoughts are really shallow! I wrote on

a Post-it, slapping it down over the picture of the brain. "Come on, Pabs. We've got to go."

We closed the journal. Pablo climbed inside the lock to pull the lever back to where it had been. Quickly I put the book back on top of the dresser, then sucked in a ton of air to produce a giccup. It worked, and by the time I had shrunk down, Pablo was already in the jeep, ready to take off.

Here's one last tip that Pablo asked me to tell you. The next time you shrink down to the size of a toe and want to shoot yourself across a room with a scrunchy, skip it. They don't really have much zing. Stick with rubber bands.

As you probably guessed, the scrunchie sling shot was a total bust. We went about two inches and then sputtered to a complete stop. What can you expect, really? Anything used to hold a girl's hair in a pony tail wasn't built for speed.

But it didn't matter. First of all, everything else on our Pablo's Perfect Phive list had been total, flat-out nonstop fun. And second of all, we had added the "Mess Up Robin's Diary" event, which easily replaced the scrunchy shot in the Top Phive List.

And besides, I ask you—who cares about a stupid scrunchy ride when you're about to blast off in a rocket?

CHAPTER 12

The Funkster's Funky Fact #12: The first successful parachute descent was made in 1797, over 100 years before the airplane. (It was from a balloon.)

Pablo and I could hardly wait for Robin to get home from school so we could see her reaction to the Post-it Notes.

Well, disappointing news. Robin called after school to say her friend Hailey had invited her to come for dinner and a sleepover, and my mom had the nerve to say it was okay. So Pabs and I were just going to have to wait until the next day to get our big laugh.

I don't mind telling you that I was pretty wiped out after our action-packed day. Pablo was too. In fact, before everyone came home, he went into his teepee and took a two-hour nap. But me, I couldn't do that. I had to look all bright eyed and bushy tailed so my mom wouldn't think I was sick. I for sure needed to be able to go to the rocket launch the next day. No kidding. I mean, when you make a list with five things to do on it, you've got to do all five, right? Otherwise, you'd just make a list with four things on it and call it a day.

So while Pablo kicked back, I got to spend the evening being on my best behavior for the Funk women. That meant playing like twenty hours of Monopoly with Goldie, and letting her win. Then being interviewed by Lark for the article she was writing on whether or not facial hair should be allowed in high school athletics.

"Male athletes should definitely be allowed to have beards," I told her. "But I think the women should only have mustaches." That cracked me up, but old Lark wasn't amused.

"Honestly, Daniel," she said. "Can't you ever be serious?"

"Listen, Larkster, no offense, but you're serious enough for both of us."

I knew that would get rid of her. After she stomped off, I did some chanting with Lola in her sweat lodge in the backyard, helped my mom change the bandages on an injured iguana's tail, and took Great Granny Nanny for a rumba spin around the living room.

Yup, just another regular Friday night in the Funk house.

I think you can understand why I was very relieved when Vu called to arrange for carpooling to the La Brea Tar Pits the next day. It was the first contact with a non-Funk-type human being I'd had all evening.

"Mom, can you drive tomorrow if Vu's parents pick us up?" I called out to her.

"Sure, honey," she answered. "Just make sure he's here by ten-thirty. I have to drop you and get home because I have Dexter's therapy session at noon."

My mom has been working with this parrot named Dexter who has a cussing problem. Every time he opens his beak, a streak of cusswords comes out. She's helping Dexter clean up his language and reduce his anger level. I don't know what he's got to be angry about. Maybe some other parrot ate all his birdseed. Whatever. I guess he's got his reasons.

I went into my room to get out my rocket and make sure everything was ready for the next day. Pablo was sitting outside his teepee, drawing with one of his pencil tips. He's a very good artist. I carried him over to my desk and let him watch while I carefully took the Screamin' Mimi out of my backpack and placed it in the center of the desk.

"Whoa," he said, looking up at the sleek black rocket. "She's a beauty."

"And she whistles when she takes off," I said.

"I better bring earplugs, then. And a parachute."

"Already done," I told him.

I took off the nose cone and showed Pablo the

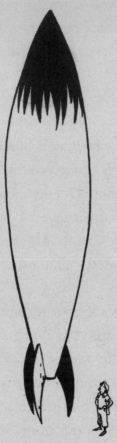

inside, where he was going to ride and where the little orange parachute was attached.

"So how do we know the parachute's going to open?" he asked.

"The motor ejects it automatically," I said. "The parachute slows the rocket's fall, and you'll glide gently back down to earth."

LIN OLIVER

"Cool, let's see the motor, dude."

"Kids don't touch the motor," I explained. "Ms. Addison puts it on just before the launch. It's got black powder in it, so she doesn't want us to get burned or anything."

"Black powder, huh?" Pablo got quiet, at least for him. "So do these things ever catch on fire?"

"Listen, Pabs, if you don't want to do this, we don't have to. We already did the first four items on our list."

I was sort of hoping he'd back down, so I could too. For the first time, it was occurring to me that being an astronaut was dangerous fun. But as I think you've figured out by now, backing down isn't my brother's style.

"It's called Pablo's Perfect Phive for a reason, dude," he said. "Sorry, no deal, Jameel."

So we made the plan. I figured that Pablo should go first. I'd put him in my rocket and watch his launch and re-entry. Then I'd know where he landed so I'd be able to find him after my ride.

I was going to go up in Vu's rocket. I was pretty sure I could shrink myself down without Vu noticing. It was his first rocket launch, and it's a known fact that during your first launch, you're so excited that you're not looking at anything but your own rocket.

I had built a Big Bertha before, so I knew how to get the nose cone off and crawl inside. The hardest part was figuring out how to giccup silently enough so the whole Science Club wouldn't stare at me.

Granny Nanny came in to say good night, and Pablo and I both thanked her for a great day.

"I had fun too," she said. "I dig the boy stuff."

We all laughed. Then we got in bed, me in my racing car bed and Pablo in his teepee. Granny gave me an air tuck, which is her specialty. She picks up the blanket and flaps it all around and then lets it go. When it settles back down on your body, it feels like the air is tucking you in. She's always told me it was my dad's favorite thing when he was a kid.

"Good night, boys," she said as she turned off the lights. "I hope you had a good bonding day."

As Pablo and I settled into the darkness, I started to feel pretty nervous about going up in space. I could feel my heart beating fast. I kept tossing and turning. I knew I was keeping Pablo up, because I could hear him tossing and turning too. His eucalyptus leaf made a crunching sound every time he rolled this way or that. They say identical twins each feel what the other one is feeling. I believe it, because after a few minutes, he said, "You okay, dude?"

"I'm a little nervous," I said. "Hey, Pablo, do you ever get scared?"

"Not much. You?"

"For the first couple years after Dad died, I was scared a lot. Scared of the dark. Scared of big dogs. Scared of being alone. Scared of being in the bathtub."

"Why? Did you have a man-eating rubber ducky?"

"I know it was stupid. But I thought I was going to go down the drain."

We both laughed, and then we were quiet again.

"He told me I didn't have to be afraid of anything," Pablo said after a while. "That he would take care of me."

"Who told you that?"

"Our dad."

I sat up in bed and flicked on the light next to my bed. Pablo was out of his teepee, standing up by the flap. He looked sad, and kind of nervous.

"I wasn't sure if I should tell you," he said.

I couldn't believe what I was hearing.

"You knew him?" I asked. "He knew you?"

"Not for long," Pablo said, walking along the bedside table so he could get close to me. "Granny told him about me when I was three."

"But that's how old I was when he . . . when he died."

"I know," Pablo said. "I only knew him for a couple of days before he went to South America. Granny introduced us before he left."

"That's cool. She wanted him to know you."

"She wanted him to find a cure for me. I think he went to look for plants in the jungle that could make me big. Reverse the shrinking."

"No, that's not why he went," I said, shaking my head. "He went to record bird sounds. Mom told me. They were looking for the rainbow-billed toucan."

"That's originally why he was going to South America," Pablo said. "But when he learned about me, he decided to take a detour and head way up river where this one special medicine plant is supposed to grow. He had never been that far up river before."

I reached out and picked Pablo up, and held him in the palm of my hand. I suspected what he was going to say next, and I knew it was going to be hard for him.

"Pablo, we don't know what happened to Dad," I said as softly and as gently as I could.

"I think I do. I'll bet he went up river looking for a cure for me and . . . that's . . . that's . . . when he . . . disappeared."

Pablo sounded like he was going to cry.

"Listen, Pabs. There's a lot of bad things that can happen in the jungle. I promise you, whatever happened to our dad wasn't your fault."

Pablo shrugged. I could tell he had been thinking about this for a long time. Maybe even for his whole life.

"Before he left, he took me in his hand," Pablo said. He was actually crying now. "I remember he had this freckle that looked like . . ."

"A bear claw," I said. Pablo nodded.

"His hands smelled like vanilla ice cream. And he told me not to be afraid. He probably said the same thing to you, bro."

I tried to remember him talking to me, the sound of his voice. But I couldn't. I could remember the vanilla ice cream, though. It was his favorite flavor. Vanilla bean, he called it. In my memory I could see the white eagle feather in his hat, too. He loved eagles because they were wild and free. Maybe that's why I never forgot that feather in his hat.

My heart was really beating fast now. And it had nothing to do with the rocket.

"I wasn't going to tell you any of this," Pablo said.

"You have to tell me everything," I told him. "We're brothers. His sons."

"I just don't want to make you sad, bro."

"You don't make me sad, Pablo. I had the best day of my life today. And tomorrow, we're going up in a rocket. Come on. Life is good. He'd be proud of us."

Pablo held up his hand, and we high-fived. When I'm big and he's little, his high five feels like a butterfly wing on my hand.

I put him down and he went back in his teepee as I turned off the light. My head was spinning, and I wanted to go to sleep. I didn't know exactly what to feel. I knew one thing, though. It was a lucky day, the day I shrank down to the size of a toe and discovered my brother.

"Good night, Pabs," I said into the darkness.

"Good night, Daniel," he said.

It was the first time he had called me by my real name.

CHAPTER 13

The Funkster's Funky Fact #13: The world's children spend five billion hours a year playing with LEGOs.

I'd like to tell you that the next day I was up bright and early, ready for the big launch. I'd really like to tell you that, but it wouldn't be true. The truth is, I overslept. The first thing I remember was my mom shaking my shoulders and saying, "Get up, Daniel. We're leaving in fifteen minutes. Vu is already here."

After she left, I sat up in bed, rubbed the sleep out of my eyes, and tried to pull my head together.

"Pablo, you up?" I muttered. "We've got to get ready."

I knew it would be hard to wake him up. He's not exactly a morning person. I stuck my finger inside his teepee to give him a poke. When I didn't feel anything, I looked inside. He wasn't there.

The PabloPhone was ringing. I picked up the straw and put it to my ear.

"I'm over here by the castle, bro," Pablo said. "Check me out."

I went to the table in the corner of my room where I used to build LEGO cities when I was younger.

There's a LEGO castle there, and sometimes Pablo plays in it. He's even slept in the turret when he's in a knights-in-armor kind of mood.

Pablo was standing in front of the castle, looking . . . well . . . let's just say . . . very unusual. On his head, he was wearing a LEGO helmet that had come with the motorcycle guy in the build-a-motorcycle kit. On his chest, he had LEGO armor that came from one of the medieval knights, only it was too big for him, so it hung all the way down to his ankles. He had put another shield on his back, and with both of them on, he looked like a LEGO clamshell. To top

off the look, he was holding a black plastic flag that was meant to fly on top of the castle.

"You like?" he said.

"Um . . . sure, Pabs. But it's kind of a bad time to be playing with LEGOs."

"I'm not playing, dude. I'm getting dressed. This is my astronaut gear."

"Oh, wow! You could have fooled me."

"Check it out, bro. The helmet to protect the noggin. Body armor to avoid broken bones. And the flag, just in case we discover a new planet. I've decided to dub it PabloLand."

I laughed. I was glad to see Pablo was in a good mood, after being so sad the night before.

"You're talking to your LEGOs?" a voice said. "That's so not normal."

I whipped around to find Vu standing in my room. My mom must have left the door open, and he just wandered in. He came over to the LEGO table and stared at Pablo. Luckily, Pablo had the good sense to stand very still so he looked like one of the LEGO toys.

"You built that guy? He's weird looking," Vu said.

I saw Pablo stick his tongue out at Vu, and I gave him a hand signal to cut it out.

"He's a medieval astronaut," I said.

"Learn a little history, Dan," Vu said. "Medieval guys rode on horses, not rockets."

"How do we know for sure?" I said. "After all, we weren't there."

I know, I know. It was a weak argument. But give me a break here. I had only been up for two minutes, and my brain wasn't really awake yet.

I picked up Pablo to get him out of sight, and I could feel him squirming in my hand.

"I'm taking him with me to the launch," I told Vu. "For good luck."

"I have a good-luck charm too," Vu said. He reached into his jacket pocket and pulled out a little pig made of green jade. Vu's family is from Vietnam, where they carve really pretty things from jade. "It's my grandmother's lucky pig. She said to rub its belly before my rocket goes up."

"That's a great idea," I said. "I'll do the same thing with my good-luck charm."

Just to emphasize the point, I rubbed Pablo's belly. He stuck his tongue out at me. I carried him over to my backpack to put him in the zipper pouch, leaving it halfway open so he could breathe.

"Tell your little pal I'm not a pig," he said to me, as I bent down to settle him into the pouch. "And nix the belly rubbing." I closed the zipper a little more. I didn't want him complaining all the way to the park.

Out in the living room, Lark was in her total reporter mode, which is one of her most irritating modes. As soon as I left my bedroom, she was in my face with her Webcam, asking a million questions no one cared about.

"Can you tell us how you feel on the morning of the launch?" she said, shoving the camera so close I thought she was trying to get a shot of the inside of my nostril.

"Excited. Nervous. All tingly inside," I said.

"Really?"

"No."

"Thanks, Daniel, for your help. I could use a real interview, you know."

I had no time for interviews, and even more important, no interest. I had exactly three minutes to eat breakfast, brush my teeth, get my permission slip signed (yup, it was late), feed Princess, put my backpack in the trunk, get in the car, and strap on my seat belt. Something had to go.

You guessed it. It was the tooth brushing.

Hey, it's a known fact that Neil Armstrong wasn't all involved in oral hygiene on the day he walked on the moon.

It's about a twenty-minute drive to La Brea Park

from our house, unless there's traffic, which there always is. So it was after eleven o'clock by the time we got there. I could see our Science Club already gathered on the lawn on the far side of the park. Robin was there with her friend Hailey.

"Just drop us off here, Mom," I said as we pulled into the parking lot. I didn't want to be any later than we were, and for my mom, looking for a parking space is a long, slow, painful process.

She pulled over and Vu, Lark, and I got our stuff out of the trunk.

"See you later," I called to her, and took off running across the grass.

Suddenly I had a thought. I was going up in a rocket. Anything could happen. Being an astronaut was dangerous work.

I turned and ran back to my mom, who was just getting back into the car. I threw my arms around her and gave her a big hug.

"I love you, Mom." I said.

Just in case anything happened, I thought she should know.

CHAPTER 14

The Funkster's Funky Fact #14: The speed required to escape the gravitational pull of the Earth is about 25,000 miles per hour.

Hancock Park is about one-third grass, one-third museum and one-third tar pits. The tar pits are black ponds of sticky tar. In the middle of the biggest pool are stone statues of prehistoric creatures. In one corner, a saber-toothed tiger and a woolly mammoth are battling some other huge creature with giant tusks. I think it's an American mastodon. Whatever it is, it's huge and scary looking. Our Science Club was gathered in a grassy flat area just on the other side of the guy with the tusks.

"Sorry we're late," I said to Ms. Addison as we came running up.

"Put your things down and join us," Ms. Addison said. "We're getting ready to launch your sister's rocket."

Robin was kneeling in the middle of the circle of kids, setting up her bright pink rocket. I noticed that she was wearing green shorts with a purple tank top, just like she had written in her journal. If you ask me,

and I know you didn't, they actually looked pretty good together. Don't ever tell her I said so, though.

"Everyone stand way back," Ms. Addison said, "and get ready for a thrill."

She bent down and put some black powder in the rocket motor. Then she lit a match to it.

Whoooosh! Robin's rocket took off straight into the air. Her rocket, which was called the Quark, was supposed to reach a height of about 700 feet. And believe it or not, I think it did. I mean, that little pink sucker went way above the trees, way above the top of the museum, even.

Robin screamed so loud that I had to put my fingers in my ears just to keep my eardrums from falling out onto the ground. They tell you to wear ear plugs at a rock concert but a rock concert is quiet, compared to the screeching that came out of my sister's mouth.

"Yo! What's all the screaming about?" Pablo said, sticking his head up out of the zipper pouch. "A guy could go deaf."

"That's Robin's rocket up there," I told him.

We both looked up just in time to see the rocket turn in the sky and start to fall back to earth. I don't know about Pablo, but when I saw that, my stomach did a nervous little flip. Okay, a big flip. But then, the nose cone blew off and the parachute ejected, just as it was supposed to. Robin got out her cell phone and started taking pictures of her rocket as it floated back to earth.

"Isn't it adorable?" she said.

I wondered if any of the scientists at NASA ever thought their rockets were adorable. Powerful, maybe. Or swift. Or accurate. But adorable?

"Robin, save those photos," Lark called. "My blog

readers will want to see them." Yeah, as if she has any blog readers.

"I'm feeling the feelings of her rocket," Lark said to me. "So alone yet so surrounded."

Honestly, folks, don't you feel sorry for me, having to listen to this kind of slobbery talk? It's not like this is a once-in-a-lifetime event. Lark jabbers about every little feeling she's ever had about anything. The other day she told me to *feel* my *feelings*. As if I was planning to do something else with them, like play hockey with them or take them to lunch.

"Was that the first launch of the day?" I asked Ms. Addison.

"The second," she said. "Vince's rocket was the first and it was quite a spectacular vehicle. It had a glide recovery system, an AstroCam digital camera and a GPS function."

Of course it did.

Vince Bruno always has the best of everything. Well, if it's not the best, at least it's the most expensive. And believe me, he lets you know how much everything costs, and follows that by telling you how cheesy your stuff is, just to make sure you feel really bad.

I was planning to flash my Screamin' Mimi in front of his pizza face. Maybe it didn't cost as much as his, but it had class. And it was made with love, not bought with his dad's money.

"Where is the old Pizza Prince?" I asked Ms. Addison.

"Oh, he's sitting over there, across the path," Ms. Addison said.

Figures. It's just like Vince not to want to participate with the group. I'm sure he was over there admiring the price tag of his GPS function. I tell you, the guy's in love with his stuff.

"Who wants to go next?" Ms. Addison asked.

I looked at Pablo, and he gave me a thumbs up.

"You sure?" I whispered.

"Let's go, Joe."

"I'll go next," I called out to Ms. Addison. Just like my mom always says when I'm trying to put off clearing the table, there's no time like the present.

I put my backpack on the grass and kneeled over it so no one could see me lift Pablo out and put him inside Screamin' Mimi's nose cone.

"Hang onto the sides until you're back on the ground," I told him as I screwed the nose cone on tight. "Good luck, Pabs."

"You call that guy Pabs?" Vu said. "I didn't know LEGO guys had names." Where had Vu come from? I was going to have to talk to him about his new habit of sneaking up on me.

"Sure," I said. "Don't you have a name for your grandma's pig?"

He shook his head.

"How about Stephanie?" I said. "I've always liked that name for a pig."

Vu gave me a strange look as I slapped him on the back and quickly headed for Ms. Addison. I was excited, but also nervous for Pablo, and I wanted to get on with the launch.

Ms. Addison packed the black powder into the engine, then put the match to it. I held my breath when the rocket took off. But I'm here to tell you, friends, it was a picture-perfect take off. I mean, those guys in the white shirts and ties at NASA couldn't have done it better. Screamin' Mimi shot up into the air, straight as a ruler, whistling like Lola's teakettle as it went. I don't want to brag, but let me just say, everyone in the park turned to look.

All I could think about was Pablo inside that nose cone. Man, I bet this was the thrill of his life. He'd never even been on a roller coaster at Magic Mountain, and there he was, shooting almost out of sight into the skies over Los Angeles. I think our dad would've been really proud of him for being so brave.

When the rocket reached the top of its trajectory,

I held my breath as it flipped and headed down to earth. Where was the parachute?

Come on, get out there! Do your thing, chicken wing!

I know you care about Pablo just as much as I do, so I'm not going to keep you in suspense any longer. Within seconds, the nose cone shot off and that little

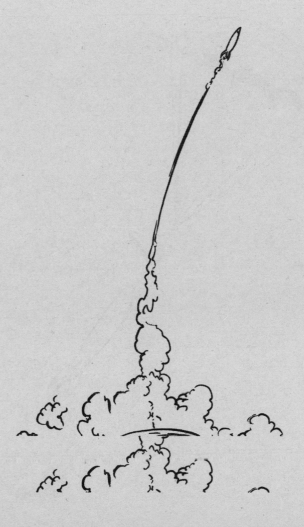

orange parachute came blasting out. It was a beautiful thing. Slowly, slowly, slowly, it carried my mini twin brother safely back down to earth.

It was a perfect Number Phive.

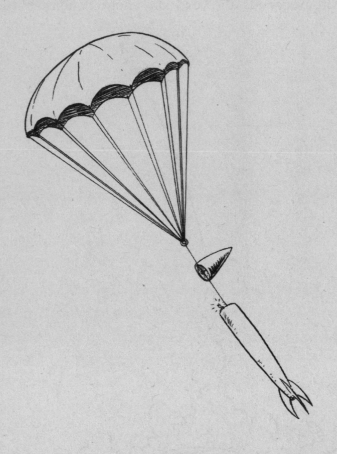

CHAPTER 15

The Funkster's Funky Fact #15: In 1985, Coke was the first soft drink consumed in outer space.

I never took my eyes off Screamin' Mimi as she floated down into the park. The nose cone, which was hanging on to the rest of the rocket by a rubber band, made a soft landing next to a short, bushy palm tree. I studied the tree and counted the leaves—there were seven of them—so I'd know exactly where to find Pablo when I went to get him. We had agreed that he would wait for me wherever he landed, because trying to find your way around the La Brea Tar Pits when you're the size of a toe is definitely a poor idea.

Meanwhile, Vu had volunteered to go next, so I had to hurry if I was going to go up in his rocket. He was with Ms. Addison and some of the other kids at the restrooms, but he'd be back soon. This was my chance and I had to grab it fast.

I got my lunch bag from my backpack and took out a hunk of Lola's Italian salami and a can of Coke.

"Don't you ever stop eating?" Robin said, as I wolfed down the salami.

"I eat until I explode," I said, "which I'm about to do. So you'd better step away if you don't want to get splattered with stomach slime."

"Eeuuww," Robin said, immediately walking as far away from me as she could.

I was about to giccup, and I didn't need any witnesses to my shrinking.

I gave the Coke can a good shake to make sure it was nice and fizzy. Then I popped the top and took big gulps of the Coke as it exploded out of the can. I drank it as fast as I could, then opened my mouth really wide. I didn't have to wait long.

A giant giccup came rolling out. It went on forever. I'm not kidding, I think it started way down in my toes.

Just as the long, loud giccup ended, a senior citizen in tennis shoes and a Dodger cap walked by.

"Excuse *you*, young man," she said, shaking her finger at me. Then I heard her say to her husband, "These kids today have no manners."

I felt bad that I had offended her. She seemed like a nice lady, and besides, anyone who's a Dodger fan is automatically a friend of mine. I wanted to apologize but there was no time for that, because I could feel the growling starting up in my eyeballs. And then came the rest.

My nose started to bubble.

My fingers began to buzz.

My knees let out a surprisingly loud whistle.

And I shrunk.

It was a weird feeling, shrinking in a public place like the park. Here I was, having an entire body-changing experience, and everyone else went on playing ball and pushing strollers and chasing their dogs, exactly as they had before. It was only me who was different.

I had planned to shrink so that I'd be right next to Vu's rocket. And I don't mean to brag, but my plan was perfect. After my head stopped spinning, I stepped right over to Big Bertha and crawled into the nose cone. Big Bertha was a big rocket, so there was lots of room for me to arrange myself comfortably inside. I sat down and pushed my feet against the wall, bracing myself so I'd stay firmly planted, no matter what.

Before long, I heard Vu's footsteps and saw his flip-flops next to me. Wow, he had huge toes! Here's a tip, friends: Do not look at the human toe too closely or you'll find all sorts of nasty things you never knew were there. If you don't believe me, look at your big toe under a magnifying glass. It's a major ick-a-thon.

Vu picked up Big Bertha and closed the nose cone so it was snug and tight. Suddenly, it was totally dark inside, and I was alone.

I'll admit it. At that moment, I would have jumped out if I'd had the chance, but there was no way I could turn back now. I wondered if Pablo's heart had been beating as fast as mine when they turned the rocket on its tail and put it in the vertical takeoff position.

I sat and waited. None of the other items on our list had made me nervous, but I confess, this one sure did.

Come on, number phive. Let's get on with it!

It wasn't long before I smelled something. What was that? It was a burning smell, like from a match. Wait a minute . . . that meant that we were about to . . .

Whoooooooooaaaaaaaaa!

The next thing I knew, I was blasting off at what felt like a million miles a second. Even though my head was up in the air, my stomach was still down on the ground. Man oh man. The speed! The thrill! The rush!

It only lasted about ten seconds, but I swear to you, it was the most exciting ten seconds of my life. There isn't even a word for how exciting it was, except maybe *totally-thrilling-spine-tingling-head-spinning-*

finger-buzzing-bubble-bursting-gut-wrenching-super-duper-all-time-fun.

Hmmm . . . I wonder if that's in the dictionary. If it isn't, they should put it in, because it's a very useful word for people flying in rockets.

I could feel the rocket tip over when we reached the top of our straight-up trajectory. That meant we were on the way down. Now was the time for the parachute to eject.

Okay, parachute. Any time now. Whenever you're ready. Come on out. No need to wait.

It wasn't coming.

Good-bye, world. It's been fun. Good-bye, Princess. You've been a good dog. So long, Brittany. I'll miss your little hamster face. Good-bye, red Porsche that I never got to buy. So long, Pabs. It's been short but sweet . . .

Wait! Suddenly, there was a blast of air in my face. Yes!

The nose cone blew off and the parachute exploded out. The gust of air filled the parachute and we went from falling at a gazillion miles an hour to floating downward at a nice gentle pace. Phew.

Hello, world. Hello, tar pits. Hello, Ms. Addison. Hello Vu, my old pal. Hello, Vince the Pizza Prince, over there by that tree. Wait a minute. I take that hello back. You don't get a hello.

I looked out at the view, and it was amazing. I saw the Page Museum, where scientists were cleaning and sorting the prehistoric fossils they had found in the tar pits. I saw the treetops in the park, and even noticed the seven-leafed palm tree where I knew Pablo was waiting for me. I saw little kids climbing on the saber-toothed tiger statue and heard their laughter. I was totally peaceful as I looked out and saw the tar pits right under me.

Wait a minute! The tar pits are right under me!

Oh, no! I was heading for the tar pits. And not any old tar pit. The big one with the woolly mammoth battling the guy with the giant tusks. What's his name . . . the American mastodon.

His sharp tusks were pointing straight up at me. If you ask me, and I know you didn't, this was definitely not a good landing spot.

CHAPTER 16

The Funkster's Funky Fact #16: Elephants are either "right tusked" or "left tusked", using one tusk more often as a tool. That tusk becomes shorter than the other one.

The bubbling tar was coming closer and closer as I floated down from the sky. I tried wiggling around inside the nose cone to see if I could throw it off course and change the landing site, but it didn't work. We were heading straight for the tar pit, no doubt about it.

I was a goner.

One day, they'd find me here, a mini fossil of a miniboy. Maybe they'd write about me in scientific journals and I'd become famous. MYSTERY MINI DUDE PUZZLES SCIENTISTS.

Wow, was I ever sorry I had made this particular choice for Pablo's Perfect Phive. What was I thinking? Minikids don't just go flying around in rockets. I should have known that trouble like this would happen.

I was in the middle of beating myself up about my stupid decision when suddenly I noticed that Big Bertha had stopped falling. We seemed to be hanging there in space, not going higher, but not going any lower either. Where was I?

I crawled along the edge of the nose cone and stuck my head out to look around. The rubber band holding the nose cone on was caught on something. When I stuck my head out a little farther, I could see that we were hanging from . . . of all things . . . the long pointy tusk of the American mastodon statue!

Three cheers for extinct animals.

I hung there from that tusk for a long time, hoping Vu would come to get his rocket. But he didn't. It was looking like I was going to spend the night, or maybe even the rest of my days, suspended over a tar pit. Pablo was the only one who even knew that I was inside the nose cone, and there was no way a mini-guy like him could help me.

Suddenly, I heard a rattling outside the nose cone. I peeked out and saw a long stick, like a fallen tree branch, coming toward me. The tip of it caught the rubber band and lifted the rocket off the mastodon's tusk. I swung back and forth in the nose cone as the stick carried me across the tar pit. A couple of times I felt like I was falling, but I shut my eyes and hung on tight until I was safely over solid ground.

I had to know who had lifted the rocket off the mastodon's tusk. Was it Vu, come to retrieve his rocket? Or a guard who worked for the park? Or maybe some nice person out playing with his dog on this sunny day?

The answer, if you're wondering, is none of the above.

A pair of hands took the rocket, put it inside a backpack and started to walk away with it. As I bounced inside the pouch, I looked around to get a clue whose backpack I was in. I could see a book called *Wise Woman Poems*. And a dark-colored sweater. And a digital camera.

Holy macaroni! I had been saved by my sister Lark.

Before I knew it, she was taking the rocket out of the backpack and putting it gently on the ground.

"I recovered your rocket, Vu," I heard her saying. "I know how much time you put into making it, so I thought you'd like to have it back."

Could this be? My sister Lark, behaving like a normal person? A nice person? A sweet person? Wow, you've got to watch out for sisters. They can surprise you when you least expect it.

This was no time for me to get all full of sisterly love, though. I had more important things to do.

I left the nose cone, pulled out a blade of grass and rubbed it lightly on the edge of my nose. "Ah choo!"

I sneezed, and before you could say Big Bertha, I was full size, standing there behind Vu and Lark. I tapped Vu on the shoulder.

"Where've you been?" he asked me. "Did you see my rocket? Man, it went really fast and high."

"So I hear," I said.

I would have paid a million dollars to tell him I had been inside it. But it's a known fact that I don't have a million of anything, let alone dollars.

"Daniel, I'd like you to go away now," Lark said. "I'm going to interview Vu and I don't want you distracting him with your stupid boy jokes."

There she was. Back to the old Lark I knew and loved.

"Ms. Addison, I'm going to retrieve my rocket," I called to her.

"That's fine, Daniel. Come right back," she said.

I hurried over to the palm tree with the seven leaves. The Screamin' Mimi was there, lying on the grass. I picked it up and looked inside, but Pablo was nowhere in sight!

I searched all around the tree, but I couldn't see him. No wonder. After all, he was shorter than the grass. I got down on my hands and knees and started feeling around.

"Did you lose something, Funk?"

Oh no. It was Vince Bruno, standing there with his big tomato-shaped head blocking out my sunlight.

"Yeah, a dime," I said. "It's here somewhere."

"A dime," he said with a laugh. "What can you buy with a dime? I spit on dimes."

He kneeled down to tie his shoelace. That was when I noticed something on his shoe. It was Pablo, waving his hands at me.

"Bro, over here," he called. At least, I think that's what he said. From where I was, his voice sounded like a baby mouse squeaking.

"Pablo!"

"I couldn't find you," he squeaked, "so I caught a ride."

"Get over here!" I said, before I could stop myself. Vince looked at me as if I had lost my mind, in addition to my dime.

"Are you talking to my shoe, doofus?"

"Of course not. I have nothing to say to your shoe. And it has nothing to say to me."

"You're weird, Funk," he said. "Too weird for me." Vince stood up and started to walk off.

"I'm out of here," he said. "My dad's taking me to lunch at the Museum Grill. My family doesn't do brown bags, you know."

"Jump!" I called to Pablo as Vince took off down the path to the museum.

"Can't," Pablo called.

Vince was walking pretty fast. I had no choice but to follow him until he stopped so Pablo could get off. He kept turning around and staring at me.

"Get lost, Funk," he said. "If you're trying to mooch a free lunch off us, you can forget it."

"I can walk wherever I want," I said.

The more I followed him, the more uncomfortable he got. I could tell by the way he hunched his shoulders and looked down at the ground. Bullies like Vince are always scared underneath. That's why they're such bullies. I was kind of enjoying myself. Just for fun, I would occasionally shoot him a crazed, creepy face when he'd turn around to see if I was still there.

When Vince got to the museum, he hurried up to a man at the door who must have been his father, because he had tomato-colored hair just like Vince and the same bad attitude. Vince whispered something to his dad, who looked me up and down like I was a worm, and then said something to the guard.

"Jump now!" I called to Pablo. I didn't know what Mr. Bruno was saying to the guard about me, but I was pretty sure it wasn't an invitation to lunch.

Good old Pabs, he did a swan dive off Vince's shoelace. I bent down, scooped him up and dropped him in my pocket. I stood up and turned to leave, knowing that the best idea was to get out of there fast. But the guard was looking right at me.

"I'd like you to come with me, son," he said.

"Oh, no thank you, sir," I said. "I'm pretty busy right now."

"It wasn't an invitation," the guard said. "This gentle-man says you've been bothering his son. Are your parents here?"

"No, my mom's operating on cats today."

Daniel Funk! Why did you say that? It has to sound weird to this guy!

"I'm sure you can handle this situation from here," Mr. Bruno said to the guard. "Come on, Vince. I'm starving."

As Vince followed his dad into the museum, he turned around, stuck his tongue out at me, and mouthed the words: Have fun, doofus!

Meanwhile, the guard was taking me by the arm.

"Let's go inside, kid," he said.

"Tell him you're not going," Pablo called up from my shirt pocket.

"Be quiet," I whispered. The guard looked from me to my pocket. He squinted his eyes suspiciously.

"I know you think I'm talking to myself," I said, "but I can explain."

"You can explain it to my boss," the guard said. "He'll be very interested."

"That Vince Bruno made all this up!" I said. "He's a real jerk."

"Really?" said the guard. "I don't think so. He gave me this."

He showed me a coupon for one free sausage pizza at any of their Pizza King restaurants.

I knew there was no arguing with a free pizza.

I just sighed as the guard put his hand on my elbow and led me through the big glass doors of the museum.

CHAPTER 17

The Funkster's Funky Fact #17: A hard-boiled egg will spin. An uncooked egg will not.

We walked past the front desk and the gift shop and into the main exhibition hall. One wall had nothing on it but hundreds of dire wolf skulls. Another display had entire skeletons of real saber-toothed tigers. And in the corner, there was a replica of a bigger-than-life woolly mammoth. Man, that guy looked big and real.

It would have been a really cool place to visit, if only I wasn't being taken to the security office. As we walked through the museum, I kept trying to come up with a story about why I was following Vince and why I was talking to my pocket.

I wasn't having much luck.

I really didn't want them to have to call Ms. Addison. She was such a nice teacher, and she'd be really disappointed in me if she thought I had caused a commotion on a field trip.

When we got to the glassed-in security office, the guard told me to take a seat.

"I'll be right back, son, and we'll get to the bottom of this. Wait here."

The minute he was gone, Pablo popped out of my pocket.

"I caught a look at this museum while we were walking," he said. "It's the coolest."

"Pablo, get serious, will you? I'm in trouble."

"With that guy? Forget him. The Pablo finds him to be one nasty GUP."

"They're probably going to call mom or Ms. Addison or something."

"No need for that, bro. Let's just get out of here."

"Pablo, you don't understand. That guy's a guard. He's got a badge and everything. I can't just get up and walk out."

"Who said anything about walking? Let's ride, Clyde. All it takes is one little giccup."

A giccup. I had forgotten! I didn't have to stay there. I could make myself disappear. Close enough, anyway.

I looked around on the desk. Bingo! It was still lunchtime and there was a half of an egg salad sandwich and a Diet Coke on the guy's desk.

Now understand, friends. I'm not a big fan of the egg salad sandwich, and this one smelled particularly stinky. But this was no time to be picky. I held my nose, took a bite of the sandwich, and gulped it down with the soda.

There were footsteps in the hall, coming closer and closer.

"Let one rip, bro!" Pablo said. "What are you waiting for?"

I opened my mouth and tried, but maybe I was trying too hard. Nothing was coming out. I was giccup-less.

Through the glass window of the office, two men came into view. One was the guard, and the other must have been the head of security. He was a very tall man in a very gray suit. He looked to me like the kind of man who eats an egg salad sandwich every day for lunch. If you ask me, and I know you didn't, that is not my favorite kind of man.

Here's a tip. If you're ever desperate to giccup and you can't get one out, lean your stomach area over the back of a chair and press really hard. If there's any gas rolling around in there, trust me, you'll push it right out.

Which is what I did.

Just as Mr. Grumpy Guard and Mr. Stinky Egg Salad turned the door handle, a short, quick giccup popped out of my mouth!

It worked.

By the time those two guys were inside, my eyes had finished growling, my nose had finished bubbling, my fingers had finished buzzing, and my knees were all done whistling.

And Pablo and I were hiding underneath a slice of white bread, tucked into that dude's egg salad. We knew they'd never find us there.

CHAPTER 18

*The Funkster's Funky Fact #18: The saber-toothed
tiger was not a tiger but a large cat. Its canine
teeth were eight inches long!*

It was fun watching those two guys search for us. They looked under the desk and in the closet and even in the file drawers. Did they think that we hid in a file drawer? Come on. It's a known fact that an egg salad sandwich is a way better hiding place than a file drawer. Use your heads, men.

"I guess he left," the guard told his boss, which shows what a swift thinker he was.

"Let's search the rest of the museum," his boss said. Hey, now there was another brilliant idea. I guess that's why he got the big bucks.

When they left, Pablo and I popped out from under the white bread.

"Nice work, bro," Pablo said, holding up his hand to high-five me. "Let's check this place out."

"I smell like egg salad," was all I could think of to say.

Pablo leaned over and took a whiff of me. "P.U.," he said. "I'll hold my nose."

"Better hold it for your-self, too," I told him, "because there's definitely an egg-salady kind of aroma swirling around you, too."

We climbed down from the desk, bouncing from drawer to drawer to drawer, the technique we had developed the day before in Lark's dresser. Then we went into the hall and waited for a ride. Pretty soon a woman in light blue tennis shoes came walking by.

"Hop on," Pablo said, grabbing her shoelace and holding out a hand for me. I grabbed his hand and he gave my arm a yank, pulling me up next to him. We climbed up to the bow, and settled in for a nice ride. There was plenty of room for both of us, because luckily, she had tied a double knot.

Revenge of the Itty-Bitty Brothers

We couldn't see all the way up to her face—it was just too far up there. I don't know exactly who she was, but I'm pretty sure she was training to be a tour guide because she walked all around the place, stopping at each exhibit and talking to a person there. That was great for us, because we got an A-plus tour of the whole museum.

And Pablo was right, it was full of cool things. I mean, the coolest things ever. Like we saw actual teeth from a saber-toothed cat (we heard her call it a cat, not a tiger). Those creatures had huge teeth and powerful jaws. I wouldn't want one of them craving me for dinner. We saw tons of other stuff too, like a skeleton of a giant ground sloth and fossils of insects that disappeared thirty thousand years ago.

The only problem was that everything went by too fast. This was the kind of museum that you wanted to spend days in. Not the kind my mom takes me to, where you look at two paintings by a couple of dead guys and then can't wait to find the candy machine.

When Ms. Blue Tennis Shoes passed the huge woolly mammoth replica, we jumped off. Here was something you couldn't just blow by. This exhibit had a button next to it, and when you pressed it, the mammoth moved like he was about to take off after you, then raised his trunk and roared, sounding very much alive.

Pablo and I jumped on that button about ten times. We took a break when a family with a very cute baby stopped to check out the mammoth. But when he roared, the baby screamed and the family beat it pretty quick. That was fine with us—more time to hit the roar button. And what was really cool was that there was no one to tell us to stop and behave ourselves, because no one could see us. Each time the mammoth would roar, we'd pretend he was chasing us, then dive for cover. It was a blast.

Pablo said that he was going to add this to his next Pablo's Perfect Phive list. Life is strange, huh? I mean, never in a million billion years would I have thought that going to a museum would make it onto my top five list of fun things to do.

We were in the middle of one of our dive-for-cover games when I heard a commotion going on over by the front desk. At first, I ignored it because we were having too much fun. But when I heard a familiar voice, I stopped playing.

"Pablo, do you hear that?" I said to him.

"Just a bunch of GUPs shouting at each other," he said. "Nothing The Pablo hasn't heard before,"

"Listen to that voice," I said to him.

It took some convincing, but finally I managed to persuade Pablo to stop playing and go see what was happening. We hitched a ride on a passing black-and-white Nike, jumping off near the front desk. Standing right there in the lobby was our guard and his boss, Mr. Stinky Egg Salad himself. Opposite him, getting all up in his face like nobody's business, was none other than my sister Robin. And next to her was my sister Lark, who was crying like a baby.

"What do you mean, you saw him and then he got away?" Robin said to the guard. "Either he's here or he's not here."

Holy macaroni—they were talking about me!

"He was bothering a nice red-haired young man, miss," the guard answered. "So we asked him to wait in the office."

"There is nothing nice about Vince Bruno," Robin said. "Unless you happen to like stuck-up blowbags."

"My guard tells me your brother was talking to his pocket," Mr. Egg Salad chimed in. "Don't you find that strange?"

"He always acts strange," Robin said. "And by the way, we happen to like him that way."

Wow. Who knew she even liked me?

"I'm sure he'll turn up," Mr. Egg Salad said. "He's

got to be here somewhere. We've had a guard stationed at the door watching for him."

"Well, that's not good enough," Lark said through her tears. "He's our brother and we're worried about him."

"Yeah," said Robin. "It would be horrible if something happened to him."

Hold onto your hats, friends, because you're not going to believe what happened next. My sister Robin started to cry. Not because she broke a pink fingernail or couldn't find her new pink earrings, but because she was worried about me. Me. Daniel the annoying. Daniel the gross. Daniel the jerk. She wanted *me* back.

I was blown away.

"I couldn't bear it if anything happened to Daniel," Lark sobbed.

Amazing! This was the second time today that I'd seen Lark behaving like a humanoid. What was going on here?

"Pablo," I said, "we've got to let them know I'm here."

"And ruin the fun?" he said. "Get hold of yourself, dude. We are basically invisible in the coolest museum in the world. Why would we blow that?"

"But they're worried about me."

"No biggie. They'll get you back. Just not now. Come on, let's go check out that saber-toothed cat."

Before I could do anything, he grabbed my arm and yanked me onto a passing brown loafer. As we headed toward the skeleton of the saber-toothed cat, I could still hear my sisters crying in the background.

CHAPTER 19

The Funkster's Funky Fact #19: The human skeleton has 300 bones at birth, but only 206 as an adult.

We jumped off the brown loafer at the skeleton of the saber-toothed tiger. Staring up at it from our tiny size, we could really feel how ferocious the saber-tooth must have been, back in the day. Even without flesh, he seemed big and strong and hungry.

"What do you want to do first?" Pablo asked. "Climb on his rib bones or swing from his teeth?"

"Your call." As exciting as these ideas were, I just couldn't get myself in the mood.

"Okay, follow me," Pablo said.

The saber-tooth skeleton was like our own personal jungle gym. We hopped from toe bone to toe bone, climbed up his feet to the ankle bone, and scaled his giant legs all the way to his rib cage. Then we leapt from one rib bone to the next until we finally stopped for a rest right in the place that would have been his belly. Looking up, you could see his back bones going all the way to his tail. In the other direction, you could see his skull in the distance and those long, sharp teeth jutting out of his mouth.

"This is awesome, isn't it?" Pablo said.

I just nodded.

"That's all you have to say?"

I nodded again.

"Talk to me, bro," Pablo said. "We promised we'd say everything, remember?"

"You're not going to like what I have to say," I said.

"Leave that to me," he answered. "You just talk."

I took a deep breath and let it flow.

"I was thinking," I began, "about when we were talking about Dad the other night. And we said that we had to always stick together because we're brothers."

"Right," Pablo said. "His sons."

"Well, they're his daughters," I said. "Robin and Lark and Goldie. And as annoying as they are, they're still our sisters. We're all his kids. And Mom's. And right now, two of our sisters are crying and we're here having fun. That doesn't feel like sticking together."

Pablo was quiet for a minute, drumming his fingers on the rib bone. It reminded me of our mom, who drums her fingers on the car steering wheel when the traffic is bad.

I knew Pablo wouldn't like what I had to say. He was a person who loved to have fun, and here I was, being a person who wanted to put an end to one of the most fun days of his life.

"Tell you what," he said at last. "Let's have this saber-toothed cat here make the decision."

Pablo stood up and turned to face the skeleton's skull.

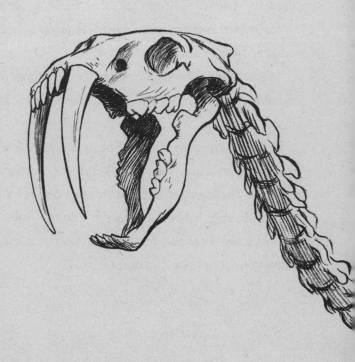

"If you think we should stay here and play with you, let me hear you roar," he shouted. "And if you think we should go back and find the sisters, then stay very quiet."

"Pabs, are you crazy?" I said. "This guy's been dead for over twenty thousand years."

"Well, then, I guess we won't be hearing him roar, will we?" he said. "So the decision is made. Let's jet, Brett."

Without another word, Pablo leaped from rib to rib, until he came to the skeleton's leg bone. He wrapped his legs around it and slid down like a fire-fighter sliding down the brass firehouse pole.

That's my brother for you. If you ask me, and I know you didn't, he's quite a guy.

CHAPTER 20

The Funkster's Funky Fact #20: Men's tear ducts are smaller than women's tear ducts.

It didn't take me long to produce a sneeze. I don't know who vacuums that museum, but whoever it is, they sure had been goofing off lately. I mean, there were some significant dustballs in that crack between the floor and the wall. I picked one up and rubbed it across the tip of my nose. Right away, my nose started kicking up a fuss, itching and tingling like crazy. I was careful not to scratch it so that when I finally sneezed, it was a huge one.

Before you could say "wooly mammoth," I had shot back up to my normal height.

"You ready?" Pablo asked.

"Yeah. Thanks, Pabs. I appreciate this."

"Let's roll, Joel."

I picked up Pablo, dropped him in my pocket, and took off running toward the front desk. As I approached, I could see that Ms. Addison was there now, and she had her arm around Lark, who was crying on her shoulder.

The guard was on a walkie-talkie. His boss was

there too, talking on a cell phone. Robin was giving him a tongue-lashing as only she can do.

"You better find my brother," she was saying, "or I'm going to make some calls. I have a cell phone, you know."

I think we all know that by now.

"Can you keep your voice down, miss?" the guard asked. "I'm checking with the parking lot attendant to see if the kid's been seen leaving the premises."

"I need to raise my voice," Robin said, "because I'm very worried about my brother. He's annoying, but he's still my brother and I happen to love him."

Wow. I almost fell over, right there on the spot.

"What seems to be the problem here?" I asked, strolling up as if nothing had happened.

"Daniel!" Robin screamed.

"You're okay!" Lark shrieked.

And get this. Both of them threw their arms around me. I mean, we're talking about a major league hug. Lark sobbed all over my shoulder.

"Easy, Lark," I said. "You'll get my shirt all snotted up."

I was glad to see her too, but I couldn't just start boo-hooing. I have my manly dignity to uphold.

"Daniel, where were you?" Lark asked, blowing

her nose in a tissue that Ms. Addison handed to her. "They've been looking all over for you."

"Can't a guy go to the bathroom?" I asked.

The guard gave me a suspicious look.

"We checked the bathrooms," he said. "You weren't in there."

"I'd show you the evidence, but I've already flushed," I said.

"Eeuuww," Robin said. "That's disgusting."

Congratulate me. It's not easy to gross out someone who's so happy to see you, but I managed, thank you very much.

"Daniel, you can't just wander away when we're on a field trip," Ms. Addison said. "I'm afraid there are going to be consequences for your actions."

"I'm sorry I worried you, Ms. Addison," I said. "I know it was wrong."

"Well, as your punishment, I'm going to have you present a report for Science Club," she said. "And when you're writing it, I want you to think about your responsibility for letting your teacher know where you are."

"I already know what I want to write about, if it's okay with you," I told her. "The skeletal system of the saber-toothed cat. I've been studying it close up."

I thought I heard a laugh coming from my pocket.

"I'll be in charge of Daniel from here on," Ms. Addison said to the guard. "I'm sorry we caused you so much trouble."

"I hope I didn't ruin your day," I said to the guard and his boss.

"It was pretty stressful," said the boss. "But I'm going to take the rest of my lunch hour to just relax. I've got a half an egg salad sandwich waiting for me on my desk."

It was all I could do to keep from laughing as we left the building.

I was wiped out by the time Mr. and Mrs. Tran arrived to take us home. It felt really good to get in their car, even though I was squished like a McDonald's cheeseburger in between Robin and Lark. Vu sat in the way back with his little brother.

"Daniel, do you want to come over for dinner?" Mrs. Tran asked, as we drove home down Pico Boulevard to Venice.

"Come on, it'll be fun," Vu said. "We can look at my pictures of the launch."

Even though I was tired, I really did want to see those pictures. I knew what Big Bertha's takeoff felt like on the inside, but I couldn't wait to see what it looked like from the outside.

"Okay," I said. "Sounds good."

"Fine. At least the house will be quiet so I can concentrate," Robin said. "I want to write down all the ideas I got today in my fashion journal."

"Uh . . . your fashion journal." I gulped. I had forgotten all about it.

"I'm going to go home and open it right up and just lie on my bed and write, write, write," she said.

Oh boy. Did I suddenly feel like a chump!

I confess, when Pablo and I were doing our Perfect Phive list, leaving the Post-it Notes in Robin's journal seemed liked a very fun thing to do. But now that I had flown in a rocket and climbed on a saber-toothed cat's skeleton, writing those notes to my sister didn't seem so fun. To be honest, I don't think it would even make it to our top twenty list. Besides, I had seen her declare her undying sisterly love for me and almost rip off that mean guard's face on my behalf. In light of that, going into her journal and leaving those notes seemed like . . . well . . . I'll just go ahead and say it . . . like a real jerky boy thing to do.

And that was no longer okay with me.

"About dinner, Mrs. Tran," I said. "I don't think I can come."

"Why?" Vu asked. "Did you make another plan in the last five seconds?"

"Actually, Vu, I did."

CHAPTER 21

The Funkster's Funky Fact #21: A toenail grows to its full length in six to twelve months.

When we got home, I made a mad dash for Robin's room. Since I didn't have the key to her journal, I knew I couldn't get it open to remove the Post-it Notes. But at least I could grab it and toss it someplace where she wouldn't find it. I was thinking Stinky Sock Mountain was the perfect hiding place. You and I both know that Robin wasn't about to go rummaging around in my already-been-worn sock pile, no matter how desperate she was to find her journal.

But a bad thing happened on the way to Robin's room.

Princess, our dog, felt the sudden need to go outside. As I was running up the front porch steps, Princess was running down them.

One thing you should know about Princess is that she has the appetite of a grizzly bear and she eats everything that doesn't eat her first. Consequently, she's built like a refrigerator. When her large body met my large feet, I went flying up in the air and came

crashing down on our porch like a sack of potatoes.
Mixed up somewhere with my legs and my backpack
and my jacket was Princess.

Robin and Lark saw this happen but weren't about to deal with it. They got out of the car and headed for the side door, leaving me there on the porch to unravel myself.

"Robin, wait up!" I called. I didn't want her to get to her room before I did.

"No way," she said. "You got yourself into that. Get out of it."

I scrambled to get back on my feet. But just as I managed to get up on one knee, I was attacked by another flying object—my sister Goldie.

"Princess!" she screamed, throwing herself out the screen door and landing on me. "You killed Princess!"

"I did not," I said. "*She* almost killed *me*."

"Let me see her!" Goldie cried. "I have to see her."

"Calm down, she's right here," I said, pulling Princess out from under my leg and patting her on the head. Her tongue was hanging out a little farther than usual, but she looked okay to me.

Goldie dropped the Ken and Barbie jeep she had been holding in her hand and threw her arms around Princess's neck.

"What's going on here?" my mom asked, coming out to the porch.

"I tripped on Princess, but she's okay," I said, trying to get to my feet so I could beat Robin to her room.

Here's a tip: If you're ever trying to swipe your sister's fashion diary, don't trip over your dog first. Because I'm here to tell you, it slows the process down. Way, way down.

"Let's have a look at you," my mom said to Princess. "Hold her still, Daniel."

"Mom, I'm in a hurry," I whined.

"Too much in a hurry to take care of an animal? I don't think so, Daniel."

What could I say? Goldie was crying. Princess was whimpering. My mom was examining her. I couldn't exactly skedaddle out of there.

Don't worry, friends. I didn't kill Princess. In fact, I didn't even hurt her. My mom checked her out, Goldie gave her a liver-flavored doggy treat, and she was back to her tail-waggy self in no time.

But the bad news is, I got to Robin's room too late.

I knocked on her door, and when she hollered, "Come in," her voice sounded weak and sad. The minute I looked at her my heart sank. She was lying on her bed, and her eyes were all red from crying. Lola was holding her hand, wiping away her tears with a handkerchief.

Oh boy. This was worse than I had thought.

"This is awful, Daniel. Just awful," she sobbed.

I searched for words to explain. I felt like a total

jerk. I confess, I even had a little lump in my throat.

"I'm sorry, Robs. I know it hurts."

"You have no idea how much it hurts," she said, breaking out into a new round of sobs.

"It will pass, honey," Lola said. "Like the Bangwa elders say, "The skies only weep until springtime comes."

"I don't care what the Bangwa elders say," Robin said, still weeping. "Daniel, can't you do something?"

"Maybe I can try to explain," I said. "I didn't mean to be such a creep. I didn't really think about how you would feel before I did it."

"Daniel, honey, I don't think you have to take it so hard," Lola said. "These things happen."

"They do?"

"Of course they do," Lola went on. "We all intend to pick up our toys, and even though it was your day to clean up, you just got a little sloppy. It happens."

Wait a minute, folks. I suddenly got the feeling we were not all talking about the same thing.

"Robin," I said, "exactly why are you crying?"

"Look," she said, sticking her foot in my face. "I tripped on Goldie's stupid Barbie jeep and stubbed my toe and broke my new jeweled sandal, too!"

Then she blew her nose really hard.

I looked down on the floor next to Robin's bed.

Her pink patent leather journal was still there. And parked next to it was Goldie's Ken and Barbie jeep. How did it get there? I had just seen it on the front porch a few minutes ago.

Pablo! Of course! Pablo had driven it in there. What a guy!

I bent down and looked closely at Robin's journal. Suddenly, I heard a little click, and the gold prongs of the lock popped open.

Pablo stuck his head out of the lock.

"It's open," he signaled with both hands.

I looked back up at Robin, and gently took hold of her foot.

"Gee, Robin, I'm really sorry you're hurt," I said.

"It's not my toe I'm crying about," she wailed. "It's my sandals. They were brand-new."

"Here," I said. "Let me see your shoe. Maybe I can fix it."

I reached out with my left hand and took her sandal. But with my right hand, I flipped through the journal and ripped off the three Post-it Notes I had stuck there.

"I bought those shoes especially to go with this outfit," Robin was saying, in her best drama-queen voice. They were nice sandals, but really, this was overkill.

"It's okay, Robs. I'm sure you'll have lots more ideas for cute outfits. Why don't you tell me some of them?"

Was this me talking? Yes, it was. Cut me a break, friends. I had to buy some time for Pablo to get in there and close up the lock.

"You really want to hear them, Daniel?"

"More than you know."

"Well, I had an inspiration today. I was thinking that maybe tomorrow I could dress all in silver, like those cute outfits the moon guys wore."

"We call them astronauts," I said, still watching Pablo fussing with the lock. "Not moon guys."

"Whatever. And maybe I'd even wear a silver beanie that looks like their helmets."

Pablo's head popped out of the lock, and he gave me a thumbs up.

"Well, I have to be going now," I said to Robin.

"But I haven't told you about the beaded hippie jeans. Or the furry pink boots. Or the tiger-striped sweatshirt," Robin said. "Now that I know you're interested, we can spend the whole night talking about fashion and reading my journal, just like you were one of my best best girlfriends."

Out of the corner of my eye, I could see Pablo getting into the Ken and Barbie jeep.

I dropped down onto my hands and knees, so Robin and Lola couldn't see me.

"Hey, you can't leave me here," I whispered to him.

"She didn't ask *me* to be her best best girlfriend," he whispered back. "You got the job, dude. Congrats."

I stood up and handed Robin her pink fashion journal. She looked so happy as she took the key from around her neck and opened it.

"Come sit next to me, Daniel. We'll start at the very beginning."

Oh, boy. Of all the things on my Wish List, this was at the very bottom. It was going to be a long, long night in the Funk house.

CHAPTER 22

The Funkster's Funky Fact #22: The giraffe has the longest tail of any land mammal. It can be up to eight feet long.

By the time I went to bed, I knew more about girls' clothes than I had ever wanted to know in my whole entire life. If you ask me, and I know you didn't, it might just be the most boring subject in the whole world. Except maybe when my Uncle Fred talks about his new weed whacker. That can get very old, very fast.

Robin seemed really happy, though, so I guess I was glad I did it.

I also had to spend a lot of the night letting Lark interview me about my feelings on the rocket launch. I told her I had so many feelings that even my feelings had feelings. Believe it or not, that made her cry, and then she ran off to her room to spread the news on her blog, www.rockets-have-feelings-too.com.

Pablo got to work right away, making our next wish list . . . Hey, wait a minute, Pablo—I'm writing this book . . .

Not anymore, bro. Hey dudes, it's the Pabs here. Mr. Sensitive was so busy feeling his feelings that he didn't have time to help me make the all-new Pablo's Perfect Phive list. So I did it myself, and I can tell you this, it's longer than a giraffe's tail. And trust me, dudes: The words "jeweled sandals" and "feel your feelings" never come up. But the words fast, fun, wicked, and wild do. So stick with me, McGee. And we'll do another phive, Clive.

Your pal,

The Pabs

Lin Oliver is the author of *Attack of the Growling Eyeballs* and *Escape of the Mini-Mummy*, the first two books in the Who Shrunk Daniel Funk? series. She is also the coauthor, with Henry Winkler, of the *New York Times* bestselling Hank Zipzer series. Lin is the executive producer of the Nickelodeon series *Wayside* as well as the writer and producer of other movies, books, and television series for children and families. She cofounded the Society of Children's Book Writers and Illustrators, of which she is Executive Director. Lin lives in Los Angeles with her husband, three sons, and one overly frisky dog. Visit her at linoliver.com.

Stephen Gilpin has illustrated numerous children's books, including the Extraordinary Adventures of Ordinary Boy series written by William Boniface. He graduated from the School of Visual Arts in New York City, where he studied painting and cartooning. He lives in Hiawatha, Kansas, with his fantastic wife, Angie, and their children. Visit him at sgilpin.com.

STEVE BRIXTON is AMERICA'S next GREAT KID DETECTIVE

(whether he wants to be or not). . . .

It all starts here: the thrilling story of Steve's first case. Our hero has a national treasure to recover, a criminal mastermind to unmask, and a social studies report due Monday—all while on the run from cops, thugs, and secret agents. We think you'll agree: Steve Brixton's first adventure is his best adventure yet.

BRIXTON BROTHERS

The Case of the Case of Mistaken Identity

"Action! Adventure! Humor! Mac Barnett has written a book kids will devour." —Jeff Kinney, author of Diary of a Wimpy Kid

Mac Barnett
with illustrations by Adam Rex

Batter Up!

Join the Travelin' Nine as they journey across the country in Sluggers, the bestselling baseball series from Loren Long and Phil Bildner.

MAGIC IN THE OUTFIELD

HORSIN' AROUND

GREAT BALLS OF FIRE

WATER, WATER EVERYWHERE

BLASTIN' THE BLUES

Make sure to catch the last inning of the Sluggers adventures, coming May 2010!

EBOOK EDITIONS ALSO AVAILABLE
From Simon & Schuster Books for Young Readers
KIDS.SimonandSchuster.com

FRANKIE PICKLE™

REALITY IS FOR GROWN-UPS!

FRANKIE PICKLE
–A NEW CHAPTER BOOK SERIES
BY ERIC WIGHT.

Published by
Simon & Schuster Books
for Young Readers